Rapture
of the
Sleep

Kevin Cunningham

Copyright © 2023 Kevin Cunningham
All rights reserved
First Edition

Fulton Books
Meadville, PA

Published by Fulton Books 2023

ISBN 979-8-88982-744-3 (paperback)
ISBN 979-8-88982-745-0 (digital)

Printed in the United States of America

Contents

Chapter 1: In the Beginning 1

Chapter 2: A Day like All the Others 17

Chapter 3: Who Are You 37

Chapter 4: Crawling from the Wreckage 50

Chapter 5: Should I Stay or Should I Go 69

Chapter 6: They Blinded Me with Science 88

Chapter 7: Is This a Dream 97

Chapter 8: Danger Is Just around the Corner...115

Chapter 9: A Different View 138

Chapter 10: Self-Discovery 158

Chapter 11: The Choice 173

Chapter 12: Return to the Nest...........................191

Chapter 13: Sharing the Gift 212

Chapter 14: Best of Both Worlds 226

Chapter 1

In the Beginning

The late afternoon sun washed the bustling streets of the city in a warm golden hue. Killian Flaherty stood outside his favorite pub, The Black Rose, nursing a glass of whiskey and watching the people pass by. He was a handsome man in his late twenties, with a confident stride and an infectious smile that effortlessly drew the attention of women. This was a game he knew all too well; his natural charm allowed him to switch from one girlfriend to another, always searching for the elusive woman who would complete him.

As the youngest son of a devout Irish Catholic family, Killian had been raised on a strong foundation of faith, hard work, and loyalty. His parents had worked tirelessly to provide their children with everything they could ever want, and it was clear that their values had been instilled into the very core of his being. Yet despite his upbringing, Killian found himself drawn to the thrill of new conquests and fleeting romances, each one leaving him more restless than the last.

"Killian!" A melodic voice called out, snapping him back to reality. He turned to see Ava, a vivacious redhead he'd been seeing for the past few weeks. She approached him with a flirtatious smile, her green eyes twinkling as she playfully swatted at his arm. "You promised me a dance tonight, remember?"

"Ah, Ava," Killian said, offering her a roguish grin. "How could I forget? You're the most captivating dancer in all the land." He took a final sip of his whiskey before setting the empty glass down on a nearby table. Taking her hand, he led her inside the pub, where a lively dance had just begun.

As they danced, Killian couldn't help but admire the way Ava's fiery curls bounced with every step, her laughter ringing like music through the air. And yet beneath the surface of his flirtations and witty banter, a nagging feeling tugged at him. His heart yearned for something deeper, more meaningful than the fleeting connections he'd grown so accustomed to.

"Killian Flaherty," Ava whispered breathlessly into his ear as they spun around the dance floor. "You've got a way with words that could charm the birds from the trees. But tell me, what is it you truly want?"

He hesitated, his eyes searching hers for a moment before he looked away. "I want…I want a love that lasts," he admitted quietly, almost ashamed of the vulnerability in his own voice. "A woman who challenges me, who makes me want to be a better man."

Ava's smile softened, and she reached up to gently touch his cheek. "Well, Killian, perhaps one day you'll find her. And when you do, I hope you hold onto her with all your strength."

As the dance came to an end and the dancers dispersed, Killian stood there, Ava's words echoing in his mind. He knew she was right. The time had come to let go of his wandering ways and seek out the love that would make him whole. Little did he know that fate had other plans in store, and soon enough, he would meet the woman who would change his life forever.

It was a crisp autumn afternoon when Killian first caught sight of her. The leaves had turned into vibrant hues of red, orange, and gold, carpeting the streets with their fiery splendor. He was sitting at an outdoor café, nursing a cup of strong black coffee and contemplating his recent decision to change his ways when she walked into his life.

"Excuse me," said the lilting voice that would soon become the soundtrack to his existence. "Is this seat taken?"

Killian looked up from his steaming mug and found himself staring into a pair of captivating hazel eyes that were greener than they were brown. They belonged to a woman who seemed to embody all the strength and beauty of a wild Cape Cod coastline. Her auburn hair was swept back in a loose braid, revealing a face that was both striking and gentle, like a fine porcelain doll.

"Uh, no," he stammered, feeling his cheeks flush with the heat of unexpected attraction. "Please, have a seat."

"Thank you," she replied, settling gracefully onto the wrought iron chair opposite him. "I'm Jennifer O'Brien."

"Killian Flaherty," he responded, extending his hand across the small table. As their fingers touched, something within him stirred, a primal recognition that this, at last, was the connection he had been seeking.

"Nice to meet you, Killian," Jennifer said, her gaze never leaving his. There was a quiet confidence about her, an inner resilience that spoke volumes about the hardships she must have weathered in her young life. And yet instead of hardening her, those experiences seemed to have given her a deep understanding of the human heart.

"Did you grow up around here?" he asked, attempting to learn more about this beautiful woman who had so suddenly appeared before him.

"Actually, no," she replied, a wistful smile playing at the corners of her lips. "I grew up in a small town a bit west of here. It was just me and my mother, sister, and brother mostly. She did the best she could, but we didn't have much."

"Your strength is evident," Killian observed, feeling an overwhelming urge to protect and care for this woman who had already captured his heart.

"Thank you," Jennifer said softly, her cheeks colored with a delicate blush. "But it's not just about me. I've always been determined to make a better life for myself and my future family."

Killian felt a pang in his chest as he locked onto her words; they resonated deep within him. As their conversation continued, he found himself more and more entranced by Jennifer, not only by her beauty but by her unwavering determination and boundless empathy.

As the sun dipped below the horizon and the world around them began to darken, Killian knew that he had found something truly special in Jennifer O'Brien. Her presence filled the void in his soul, and her laughter brightened even the deepest shadows of his heart. In her arms, he discovered a love that would burn like the eternal flame, leading him forward toward a future filled with joy, passion, and endless possibility.

The first sign of spring was in the air, and Killian and Jennifer strolled hand in hand through the park, their love for each other blooming as vibrantly as the flowers that surrounded them. Each step they took together seemed to weave an unbreakable bond, and after only six months, they knew in their hearts they were destined for each other.

"Have you ever seen anything so beautiful?" Jennifer asked, her eyes sparkling with wonder as she gazed at the cherry blossoms that lined the path. The delicate petals danced in the breeze, showering the couple in a soft pink rain.

Killian squeezed her hand gently and smiled. "Not until I saw you," he replied, his voice filled with warmth and admiration. Jennifer's cheeks flushed like the roses that dotted the nearby bushes, and Killian felt a surge of pride at having caused such a reaction in her.

As they continued their walk, Killian's mind raced with thoughts of their future together. He envisioned a quaint cottage, nestled in the suburbs, its walls adorned with the laughter and memories of their life together. The image of Jennifer, cradling a newborn in her arms, filled him with a sense of purpose and a fire that could not be extinguished.

"Jennifer," he began to say, his heart pounding in his chest. "I've been thinking…about us, our future."

Jennifer looked up at him, her hazel eyes shining with curiosity and anticipation. "Yes?" She prompted gently, her fingers intertwining with his.

"Would you do me the honor of becoming my wife?" Killian asked, his voice barely more than a whisper.

Tears filled Jennifer's eyes as she nodded vigorously, too moved to speak. They embraced, the promise of forever sealed within that simple gesture. From that moment on, their fates were entwined, their love a beacon that would guide them through every challenge life would bring.

Soon after their marriage, the couple welcomed not one but three beautiful children into their lives. Each child was a unique reflection of the love between Killian and Jennifer—the oldest, a son, Casey, who charmed everyone he met with his quick wit and ability to entertain all around him; the middle child, another son, Joe, with a big heart, who was wise beyond his years and could find the goodness in all he was around; and the youngest, a daughter, Hannah, with her mother's tenacity and her father's nurturing spirit, who could light up any room she entered.

As the Flaherty family grew, so too did Killian and Jennifer's love for each other. The challenges of raising their young brood only served to strengthen their bond, as they faced each obstacle hand in hand. And through it all, Killian never forgot that fateful day in the park, when he had first dared to dream of the life they now shared. In the quiet moments before sleep claimed him each night, he marveled at the beauty of their journey and whispered a silent prayer of gratitude for the woman who had changed his world forever.

The sun dipped below the horizon, casting a warm glow over Killian's face as he stood in the doorway of their modest home. His eyes wandered across the small living room filled with colorful toys and scattered crayons, the evidence of three young children. He couldn't help but smile as his gaze fell upon Jennifer, who was sitting on the floor, helping their youngest daughter stack wooden blocks.

"Higher, Mommy!" she squealed, her eyes twinkling with excitement.

"All right, let's see if we can reach the sky," Jennifer replied, her laughter mingling with the happy chatter of their children.

Having had their children so early in their marriage, Killian and Jennifer never had the chance to share life experiences like travel or weekend getaways that other newlywed couples typically enjoyed. There were no exotic vacations or romantic dinners by candlelight; instead, their days were filled with dirty diapers, sleepless nights, and endless rounds of board games.

Yet despite these challenges, there was something undeniably beautiful about the life they had built together. Their home was a haven of love, where laughter echoed off the walls, and each new day brought a fresh opportunity for growth and discovery.

"Look, Dad! Our tower is taller than me!" Hannah exclaimed, waving Killian over. He stepped into the room, the floorboards creaking softly beneath his feet.

"Wow, that's amazing!" he said, kneeling down and wrapping his arm around Jennifer's waist, feeling her warmth against his side. "You two make quite the team."

Jennifer leaned her head against Killian's shoulder, her eyes shining with pride as their little girl clapped her hands in delight. "We do, don't we?" she said, pressing a soft kiss to his cheek.

In moments like these, the absence of grand adventures seemed insignificant. For Killian, there was no greater joy than watching his children grow, their personalities blossoming under Jennifer's loving guidance. And as he looked into her eyes, those vibrant, unwavering pools of color, he knew that the love they shared was more precious than any worldly experience.

"Hey," Killian whispered, pressing a gentle finger to Jennifer's chin and tilting her face toward his, "I love you. You know that, right?"

"Of course I do," she replied with a tender smile. "And I love you too, more than anything in this world."

"Promise me that we'll always face our challenges together," he said, his heart swelling with emotion. "No matter what life throws at us, we'll stay strong for each other and our family."

"Forever," she agreed, sealing their vow with a lingering kiss.

As Killian held Jennifer close, surrounded by the joyful chaos of their young family, he couldn't help but feel that they had already built a lifetime's worth of memories. The road ahead might be uncertain, but one thing was clear: their love would guide them through every challenge, just as it always had.

The rain pattered gently against the windowpane, casting a melancholy glow over the small apartment. Killian sat at the kitchen table, his fingers drumming nervously on its wooden surface as he scrutinized the stack of bills before him. Jennifer stood by the stove, stirring a pot of soup, her eyes flickering between the simmering liquid and their three children playing in the living room.

"Jen," Killian began hesitantly, swallowing the lump in his throat. "I don't know how we're going to make ends meet this month."

Jennifer bit her lip, worry etched deep into the lines of her face. "We'll find a way, Killian. We always do," she replied softly, her voice barely audible above the laughter of their children.

"Maybe I should take on a second job," he suggested, his chest tightening with anxiety. "I can work nights or weekends—anything to bring in some extra cash."

"Killian, you're already working twelve-hour days," Jennifer protested, setting down her spoon and crossing the room to place a gentle hand on his shoulder. "You're exhausted enough as it is. We'll figure something out."

"Maybe if I hadn't been so insistent on staying at my comfortable job dreaming it would grow into something more, we wouldn't be in this mess," he muttered bitterly, guilt gnawing at the edges of his thoughts. "I should have taken a more rewarding job in a bigger company, something that would have provided for our family."

"Your dreams are what brought us together, Killian," Jennifer reminded him, her eyes shining with conviction. "And I believe in you, even when things seem impossible."

"Thank you, Jen," he whispered, intertwining his fingers with hers. "I promise, I'll do whatever it takes to give you and the kids the life you deserve."

They stared into each other's eyes, their mutual resolve forming an unbreakable bond. With renewed determination, Killian took a new a job at a large technology firm. He spent countless hours refining his skills, pushing himself to excel in every aspect of his role. His dedication did not go unnoticed, and before long, he was offered a promotion to managerial level.

"Jen, can you believe it?" Killian exclaimed as he burst through the door one evening, his face flushed with excitement. "They're making me a manager! We'll finally have a little breathing room when it comes to our finances."

Jennifer enveloped him in a tight embrace, her eyes shining with pride. "I always knew you could do it," she whispered, tears of relief streaming down her cheeks. "You've worked so hard for this, Killian. You deserve every bit of success."

As the years passed, Killian continued to climb the corporate ladder, driven by the love and support of his family. The small apartment that had once felt suffocating was replaced by a small home just outside the city that Jennifer transformed into a sanctuary, a testament to the strength of their bond. And though they still faced obstacles, both financial and emotional, Killian and Jennifer's love remained unwavering, guiding them through each challenge with steadfast determination.

"Look how far we've come," Killian mused one evening, his arm wrapped securely around Jennifer as they gazed out at the city skyline from their cozy living room. "All because we believed in each other."

"Love can conquer anything," Jennifer whispered, resting her head against his chest. "And I wouldn't trade our journey for the world."

In the end, it wasn't the money or the success that made their lives complete; it was the lessons they'd learned and the love they'd shared that truly defined their happiness. And as Killian held Jennifer close, listening to the distant laughter of their children, he knew that they had built something far more precious than any fortune could provide: a life forged in love, resilience, and unwavering commitment.

Killian's fingers tapped rhythmically against the steering wheel as he drove through the city streets, his thoughts consumed by the latest project he'd been tasked to oversee. The weight of responsibility pressed down upon him like a granite boulder, driving him to spend long hours at the office in pursuit of success.

"Killian, love? Are you still with me?" Jennifer's voice drifted through the car like a gentle breeze, pulling him from his daydream.

Blinking away the fog of work-related musings, Killian offered her a smile. "Sorry, Jen. Just got a bit lost in my thoughts."

"Your work will still be there tomorrow," she reminded him gently. "But tonight, it's just us and the kids."

As they pulled into the driveway of their modest home, the front door burst open to reveal their three young children, Casey, Joe, and Hannah, racing out to greet them. Jennifer's face lit up with joy as she scooped up their youngest, while Killian ruffled the hair of the older two, his heart swelling with pride.

"All right, munchkins," Jennifer called, ushering the excited children inside. "Time for dinner!"

While the Flaherty family gathered around the table, laughter and conversation mingling with the aroma of home-cooked food, Killian couldn't help but feel a twinge of guilt. He knew that Jennifer had taken on the lion's share of parenting duties in recent years, her days a whirlwind of school runs, doctor's appointments, and countless other tasks that kept their household running smoothly.

"Mom, can you help me with my science project?" Hannah asked eagerly, her eyes shining with anticipation.

"Of course, sweetheart," Jennifer replied, brushing a strand of hair behind her ear. "Just let me finish cleaning up, and we'll get started."

As she deftly cleared the table, Killian's gaze lingered on his wife, admiration and gratitude coursing through him. She was the rock upon which their family was built, her unwavering support allowing him to focus on his career and carve a path toward financial stability. And though he longed to be more present, he knew that Jennifer's strength and resilience were what kept their family whole.

"Jen," Killian whispered quietly as they settled into bed later that night, tracing the curve of her cheek with his thumb. "You've been amazing, you know. I couldn't have done any of this without you."

"Killian, love," she whispered, pressing a tender kiss to his lips. "It's not about who does what or how much we each contribute. It's about being a team, supporting each other through thick and thin."

"Still," he insisted, wrapping an arm around her waist. "I promise, I'll do my best to be there for you and the kids more. You deserve it."

"Your heart is always with us," she replied softly, her eyes shining with love. "And that's all that matters."

As they drifted off to sleep, their bodies entwined and their hearts beating in unison, Killian vowed to honor his promise, to be the husband and father his family needed. For while success was a worthy pursuit, it was the bonds of love that truly mattered, a lesson he would carry with him through the years to come.

Fifteen years later, the morning sun cast a warm glow on the Flaherty household, illuminating the rich colors of the family photographs lining the hallway. The passage of time had etched itself onto Killian's face; crow's feet danced at the corners of his eyes, which were now framed by graying hair. Yet the warmth of his smile remained unchanged, as did the love that burned fiercely in his heart for Jennifer and their children.

"Happy anniversary, love," Killian whispered into Jennifer's ear as she stirred from her slumber, her brown locks splayed over the pillowcase like an autumn canopy. He pressed a gentle kiss to her temple, feeling the familiar shape of her skull beneath his lips—a connection that had only deepened through the years.

"Is it really fifteen years already?" she whispered, her voice thick with sleep. Her eyelids fluttered open to meet his gaze, the corners of her mouth curving into a knowing smile.

"Feels like just yesterday we said our vows," he admitted, his thumb tracing tender circles on the back of her hand. "And yet we've been through so much together."

"Life has its challenges," she agreed, her fingers tightening around his. "But we've faced them side by side, and look how far we've come."

"Indeed," Killian mused, remembering the early days when they struggled to make ends meet, when Jennifer shouldered the weight of raising their three beautiful children, while he worked tirelessly to climb the corporate ladder. Their love had been tested, but it emerged stronger, forged in the fires of adversity.

"Sometimes, I worry," Jennifer confessed softly, her eyes searching his, "that the paths we walk may diverge, that our opinions might clash."

"Darlin', we're human," he reassured her, a chuckle rumbling deep within his chest. "Differences are only natural, but it's our love that binds us together."

"Thank you for understanding." She sighed, resting her head on his shoulder as they lay entwined in the cocoon of their shared memories.

"Always," he promised, sealing the words with a tender kiss to her forehead.

As the sun continued its ascent, bathing their bedroom in golden light, Killian and Jennifer reveled in the sanctuary of each other's arms. Despite the years that had passed, their love remained true, a testament to their unwavering commitment and the strength of the bond they had forged. They knew that challenges would continue to arise, but together, they would face them, hand in hand, hearts united in an unbreakable embrace.

Chapter 2

A Day like All the Others

The rain pattered softly against the windowpane as Killian, a hardworking and dedicated family man, gazed at the photograph on his desk. The glass frame protected the image of his wife, Jennifer, smiling radiantly, her arms wrapped around their three children: Casey, Joe, and Hannah. Their laughter and joy seemed to seep from the photograph, warming his heart with each glance. The desk itself was a monument to efficiency, papers neatly stacked in trays, the computer humming quietly in the corner, and pens standing like soldiers at attention.

"Mr. Flaherty," the intercom buzzed, "Emily from Finance is here for your 1:00 p.m. budget review."

"Thank you, Susan," Killian replied, his voice steady and kind. He straightened his tie and stood up, preparing himself for another meeting in his role as manager in a large technology firm in the heart of the city. His office was spacious, with a wall of windows that allowed him to gaze out at the bustling streets below. The glass buildings surrounding him reflected the gray skies in a kaleidoscope of monochromes, echoing the thoughts that buzzed throughout the city.

"Come in," he called out when there was a knock on his door.

"Morning, Mr. Flaherty," said a young woman with a stack of files in her hands. She placed them onto his desk with caution, glancing nervously at him.

"Please call me Killian," he said gently, trying to put her at ease. "What do we have today, Emily?"

"Um, well," she stammered, flipping through the files, "we've got the quarterly reports to review, some budget proposals, and a few staffing issues."

"All right." Killian nodded, sitting back down at his desk. The computer screen flickered to life as he began to sift through the digital folders. "Let's start with the budget proposals."

"Sure thing, Mr. Fl—I mean, Killian," Emily corrected herself. She pulled out a chair across from him and opened the first file, her hands shaking slightly.

As they worked through the documents together, Killian's mind wandered briefly to his family. He could imagine Jennifer in their cozy kitchen, making breakfast for the children as they hurriedly got ready for school. A soft smile played on his lips, but he quickly refocused on the task at hand.

"Killian, do you think we should allocate more funds to the server reduction project?" Emily asked.

"Perhaps," he replied thoughtfully. "But let's see if there are any other areas where we can make cuts first. Remember, it's all about finding balance."

"Right," she agreed, nodding vigorously.

The rain continued to fall outside, drumming a gentle rhythm against the windowpane. The world seemed to slow down, even if just for a moment, as Killian immersed himself in his work, always striving to provide the best for his family and those who depended on him.

Later in the day, Killian stood at his office window, watching the bustling streets below. The morning had been productive, and he felt a sense of accomplishment as he mentally reviewed the progress made with Emily on the budget proposals. Time was of the essence, but there was no denying that life, his home life, held just as much importance to him.

"Killian," a voice called out from the doorway, breaking his trance. It was Jack, one of the junior employees. His eyes were wide with anxiety, betraying the weight of some problem resting on his shoulders.

"Jack, my friend, what can I do for you?" Killian asked, his gaze never leaving the window.

"Uh, well—" Jack hesitated, shifting nervously. "I'm having trouble with my latest project, and I was hoping you could help me."

"Of course," Killian replied, turning to face Jack with a reassuring smile. He knew all too well that life's challenges often spilled into work, and he was always willing to lend a guiding hand. "Why don't you tell me what's going on?"

"Okay." Jack sighed, taking a seat opposite Killian's desk. "It's just…my girlfriend and I are going through a rough patch, and it's affecting my work. I don't know how to balance everything."

Killian nodded knowingly and leaned back in his chair, fingers steepled in contemplation. "First things first, Jack. It is important to remember that life provides us many blessings, with work simply being a distraction. You should never have to say 'Honey, not now, I have work to do.' You must embrace all the blessings in your life and focus your attention there and only worry about the issues from work that impact your life."

"Right," Jack responded, finding solace in Killian's words. He could see the wisdom etched in the lines of Killian's face, the kind eyes that seemed to hold an ocean of understanding.

"Having said that," Killian continued, "don't forget that life is precious, and you must learn to balance your work with the things that truly matter. This will not only benefit you but also those around you."

"Thank you, Killian," Jack said, his shoulders visibly relaxing. "I'll try my best to apply what you've told me."

"Good." Killian nodded approvingly, a hint of a smile playing at the corners of his lips. "And remember, if you need more guidance, don't hesitate to reach out."

"Will do," Jack promised, standing up to leave.

"Jack," Killian called out just as he was about to exit the room. "Always be willing to take on challenges in both work and life—it shows your passion for personal success."

"Absolutely," Jack replied, his face flushed with newfound determination. He then left Killian's office, eager to confront the hurdles that lay ahead.

As the door clicked shut, Killian couldn't help but feel a swell of pride. It was moments like these that made him appreciate the delicate dance between life and work, the balance that gave meaning to every step taken along the path of leadership. And with each stride forward, his passion for personal success only grew stronger.

Killian closed the day with a team meeting as he always does on Friday afternoons. As he sat in the dimly lit conference room, he saw raindrops streaking down the vast window behind him. He watched the droplets race each other like horses on a track, their zigzagging paths mirrored in his thoughts.

"Okay, folks," Killian said, clapping his hands together to get the attention of his team, who were gathered around the large mahogany table. "I know it's been a rough week, and the end of the quarter is fast approaching."

The room was filled with uneasy glances, hushed sighs, and the tapping of pens against paper. The tension hung in the air like a dense fog, smothering the space and leaving everyone feeling suffocated.

"However," Killian continued, leaning back in his chair, "we need not dwell on what we haven't done so far. Instead, let's focus on what we have accomplished and how we can pull together and push through any remaining obstacles as a team."

He paused, his eyes scanning the faces before him—some etched with worry, others with determination. He could see that they needed something more than just words of encouragement.

"Here's a little joke to lighten the mood," he said, his voice dropping a few octaves and adopting a mock-serious tone. "What do you call a group of people who are all drowning in paperwork?"

The room remained eerily silent, everyone waiting for the punchline with bated breath. Killian grinned, eyes sparkling with mischief, as he delivered the answer: "An office pool!"

A few nervous chuckles broke out, and the anxious energy seemed to dissipate slightly. Killian knew his timing was questionable, but using humor to break the tension had always been one of his go-to strategies.

"All right," he said, the grin still lingering on his lips, "let's dive back into it. We'll make sure that everyone has their roles clear, and we'll reconvene early next week to discuss our progress. Remember what I always say, a team in corporate America is no different than one of your favorite sports teams. Each player on the team has a specific role, but the only way to win the game is for all players to work together like a symphony to score the winning points. Now, go enjoy the weekend with your loved ones, and we will regroup on Monday."

As the team members dispersed, Killian remained seated at the head of the table. His thoughts drifted back to the racing raindrops, their chaotic dance a reflection of the challenges he faced daily—both in work and life.

"Leadership is taken, not given," he muttered to himself, the familiar mantra grounding him and preparing him for whatever lay ahead. With renewed determination, Killian rose from his chair and strode back to his office, ready to tackle the storm outside and within.

On his ride home, the rain had dissipated, and the sun slowly dipped low over the horizon, casting a warm glow on the idyllic city neighborhood. Killian's black Audi RS5 eased into the driveway of his comfortable middle-class home. The rhythmic crunch of gravel beneath the tires signaled his return to the place where he found solace from the daily grind.

"Hey, Dad!" Casey, his eldest son, greeted him with an enthusiastic wave as he stepped out onto the front porch. A genuine smile formed on Killian's face, his eyes shining with love for his family. His wife, Jennifer, emerged from behind the screen door, with Joe and Hannah following closely behind.

"Hey, kiddos," Killian said, fondly ruffling Casey's hair and pulling his two younger children in for a tight hug. "How was school today?"

"Great!" Joe chirped, while Hannah nodded her head vigorously. Their excitement was infectious, and Killian couldn't help but grin even wider.

"Dinner is almost ready," Jennifer informed him, leaning in for a tender kiss that never failed to bring a flutter to his chest. "Why don't you go unwind from work?"

"Sounds good." Killian agreed, giving Jennifer's hand a gentle squeeze before heading inside.

As a manager at a large technology firm in the heart of the financial district in the city, Killian's life was filled with numbers, spreadsheets, and deadlines. But each evening when he returned home, it was clear that his true calling was being a dedicated husband and father. He took great pride in providing stability and comfort for his family, ensuring that their home was always a sanctuary where they could thrive.

As dinner went on and conversation flowed, Killian couldn't help but feel a sense of fulfillment wash over him. He had worked hard to achieve this life—the beautiful home, the loving wife, and the happy, healthy children. In the quiet moments spent gathered around the dinner table, he was reminded that it was all worth it.

And yet as night fell and the children were tucked into bed, Killian found himself seated on the edge of the mattress, in deep thought. He gazed at the digital clock on the nightstand, its red numbers glowing softly in the darkness. 11:11, it read—always an auspicious moment for making a wish.

"Everything okay, love?" Jennifer asked softly from her side of the bed, concern etched in her words.

"Of course," Killian reassured her, offering a gentle smile. "Just thinking about work."

"Try not to let it keep you up too late," she advised with a soft kiss on his forehead. "Good night, my love."

"Good night," he whispered back, watching as her eyes drifted closed, her breathing growing steady and rhythmic.

In truth though, Killian's thoughts were far from his job or the comfortable middle-class lifestyle he had worked so diligently to maintain. Instead, his mind raced with thoughts of another life he had once lived; vague visions of a woman named Lindsay and the memories they shared together had begun to find their way into his waking thoughts.

The early morning sun filtered through the white lace curtains, casting a warm golden glow over the Flaherty family kitchen. The scent of freshly baked bacon mingled with the sweet aroma of cinnamon rolls, as Jennifer carefully placed a tray of them on the table. Her warm smile and gentle demeanor were the embodiment of love and devotion to her cherished family.

"Morning, Mom," mumbled Casey, shuffling into the kitchen, still rubbing the sleep from his eyes.

"Good morning, sweetheart," Jennifer greeted her eldest son, pulling out a chair for him at the breakfast table. "Your father will be down soon, and your brother and sister should be up any minute."

After a few moments, the sound of footsteps thumping down the stairs announced the arrival of Joe and Hannah, their faces lighting up at the sight of their favorite breakfast treat. Killian followed close behind, his tie slightly askew as he leaned down to give Jennifer a quick kiss on the cheek.

"Morning, darling," he whispered, pressing a hand to the small of her back before taking his seat at the head of the table.

"Morning, love," Jennifer replied, her eyes crinkling at the corners as she smiled warmly at him.

As they ate, Jennifer shared stories of her recent volunteer work at the local church, where she led a weekly prayer circle and organized community outreach programs. Spirituality was a significant part of her life, and she took great pride in using her faith to connect with others and give back to her community.

"Mrs. Jenkins from next door stopped by yesterday," Jennifer mentioned between bites. "She wanted to thank us for helping her with her groceries last week. She said she's planning to bring over some homemade jam as a token of appreciation."

"Ah, Mrs. Jenkins's famous jam." Killian chuckled. "Well, tell her we're always happy to lend a hand."

The Flaherty's neighborhood was a tight-knit community, characterized by tree-lined streets, meticulously maintained lawns, and friendly neighbors who waved hello as they passed by. In the evenings, children could be seen playing games of kickball in the street while parents gathered on porch swings to catch up on the day's events.

"Mom, can I go play at Sarah's house later?" Hannah asked, her eyes pleading with excitement.

"Of course, honey," Jennifer agreed, brushing a strand of hair from her daughter's face. "Just make sure you're home in time for dinner."

"Thanks, Mom! You're the best!" Hannah beamed, giving Jennifer a quick hug before rushing off to get ready.

As the rest of the family finished breakfast and began preparing for their day, Killian couldn't help but marvel at the life he and Jennifer had built together. Their home was a sanctuary filled with love, laughter, and warmth—a testament to the unwavering devotion they had for one another and their children.

"Have a good day at work, Killian," Jennifer said, pressing a soft kiss to his lips as he prepared to leave. "I'll be here holding down the fort."

"Thank you, love," he whispered, his heart swelling with gratitude. "I don't know what I'd do without you."

With that, he stepped out into the crisp morning air, pausing for a moment to take in the picturesque scene of city bliss surrounding him. As he walked to his car, he waved to Mr. Jefferson across the street, who was watering his rose bushes, and exchanged pleasantries with Mrs. Patel, who was walking her dog along the sidewalk. The comforting familiarity of it all brought a contented smile to his face, and he felt truly blessed to be a part of such a supportive and loving community.

The morning sun cast long, streaking shadows across the street as Killian climbed into his car, the scent of freshly mown grass hanging in the air. He turned the key in the ignition, and as the engine hummed to life, he caught sight of his own reflection in the rearview mirror. For a split second, his mind inexplicably conjured up an image of a beautiful woman with golden hair and piercing chestnut brown eyes, a face he somehow knew yet had never seen before.

"Who are you?" he muttered under his breath, shaking his head to dismiss the phantom vision. But as he pulled away from the curb, the woman's face remained etched in his mind, her name forming on his lips without conscious thought: "Lindsay."

Throughout the day, the visions persisted, each one growing more vivid and detailed than the last. Killian found himself experiencing snippets of another life, one where he and Lindsay shared a cozy cottage in a coastal town in the Carolina's, laughing over candlelit dinners and stolen kisses beneath the moonlight. The memories came to him unbidden, leaving him feeling both confused and intrigued.

"Flaherty, did you finish those reports?" his boss asked, snapping Killian out of his daydream.

"Uh, yes, sir," he stammered, suddenly realizing he'd been lost in thought for longer than he'd intended. "I'll have them on your desk shortly."

"Good man," his boss replied, clapping him on the shoulder before walking away.

As Killian sat at his desk, he couldn't help but grapple with the strange, unsettling emotions that accompanied these mysterious visions. Inwardly, he questioned why they were happening now, after so many years of contentment with Jennifer and their children. And even more troubling was the undeniable connection he felt to Lindsay, despite having no recollection of her outside of these fleeting glimpses.

"Hey, Killian," his coworker Mike said as he peered into Killian's office. "You seem a bit distracted today. Everything all right?"

"Uh, yeah," Killian replied, forcing a smile. "Just got a lot on my mind, I guess."

"Here," Mike said, handing him a fresh cup of coffee. "Maybe this will help. You know what they say, 'Coffee is the manager's best friend.'"

"Thanks, Mike," Killian said, taking a sip of the hot liquid and hoping it would clear his head. But even as he continued to sort through spreadsheets and performance reports, Lindsay's face haunted him, her eyes filled with a mixture of longing and sadness that tugged at his heart.

As the workday drew to a close, Killian found himself torn between his loyalty to his family and the inexplicable pull he felt toward Lindsay. He knew he needed to focus on the life he had, the one he loved—but how could he ignore the tantalizing glimpses of another existence? And why did the thought of Lindsay leave him feeling so profoundly unsettled?

"Time to go home," he whispered to himself, shutting down his computer and gathering his belongings. As he stepped out into the cool evening air, he resolved to put the visions behind him, to devote himself fully to Jennifer and their children. But deep down, he couldn't shake the feeling that the mysterious woman named Lindsay was somehow indelibly intertwined with his own destiny.

Killian hesitated at the door of their beautiful city home, its warm lights spilling onto the neatly trimmed lawn. He gripped the handle tightly, feeling the cold metal press against his skin—a sensation that anchored him to the present moment. Inside, he could hear the sounds of his family's laughter and the soft melodies of Jennifer's favorite music.

"Come on, Killian," he whispered to himself, fighting the strange longing that threatened to pull him away from all that he cherished. "This is your life."

He opened the door and stepped inside, the familiar scent of home washing over him like a comforting embrace. Jennifer stood in the kitchen, her auburn hair catching the light as she stirred a pot of steaming soup. She glanced up at him with a warm smile, her deep hazel eyes filled with love and devotion.

"Hey, you're home!" Jennifer said, wiping her hands on a dish towel. "How was your day?"

"Busy, as usual," Killian replied, attempting to sound cheerful. But even as he spoke, images of Lindsay flashed through his mind—her golden hair cascading down her back and the way her chestnut brown eyes sparkled with mischief. He shook his head, trying to dispel the visions, but they clung to him like shadows.

"Something smells delicious," he added, hoping to distract himself from the onslaught of conflicting emotions.

"Thanks." Jennifer beamed, clearly pleased by the compliment. "I thought I'd try a new recipe I found on the Internet tonight. How about you go check on the kids while I finish up here?"

"Sure thing," Killian agreed, grateful for the reprieve. He navigated the familiar hallway, pausing outside Casey's room to listen to the hum of his guitar, then moving on to Joe's where the rhythmic tapping of a keyboard signaled another gaming session. Finally, he reached Hannah's door, cracked open just enough for him to see her sitting cross-legged on her bed, engrossed in a book.

Everything seems in order, he thought, trying to push away the lingering visions of Lindsay. He knew he should be content with the life he had—a loving wife, three amazing children, and a stable job—but the curiosity gnawed at him like an itch he couldn't reach.

"Killian." Jennifer's voice startled him out of his thoughts, and he turned to find her standing behind him, concern etched across her delicate features. "Is everything okay? You seem…distracted."

"Sorry, I'm just…tired," he lied, forcing a smile. "Long day at the office."

Jennifer studied him for a moment, her eyes searching his face as if trying to read his soul. "If you need to talk about anything, you know I'm here, right?" she said softly, reaching out to touch his arm.

"Of course," Killian replied, his heart swelling with love and gratitude for this incredible woman who had stood by his side through thick and thin. "I appreciate that, Jen. You always know how to make me feel better."

"Good," she said, smiling back at him. "Now, go wash up for dinner. It's almost ready."

As Killian moved toward the bathroom, the weight of his inner turmoil seemed to lessen ever so slightly. He knew that he could not afford to let his curiosity about Lindsay jeopardize what he had with Jennifer and their children. Silently, he vowed to bury the visions deep within himself, to lock them away where they could do no harm.

But as he stared into the mirror, water dripping from his freshly washed hands, he couldn't help but wonder if fate had other plans.

Killian sat in his armchair, absently staring out the window. The vibrant sunset cast warm hues across their home, bathing the children's toys in a soft golden glow. He could hear Jennifer in the kitchen, asking Hannah to help set the table for dinner.

"Killian?" Jennifer called from the doorway, her voice filled with concern. "Are you ready to talk yet?"

He turned to face her, realizing that he couldn't keep his secret any longer. It was eating away at him, and he could see the worry in Jennifer's eyes. She deserved to know the truth.

"Jen," he began, "there's something I need to tell you. Something strange has been happening to me recently."

Jennifer took a step closer, her hands clasped together in front of her. "What is it? You can tell me anything, you know that."

He hesitated for a moment before speaking, his heart pounding in his chest. "I've been having these visions of another life, one where I'm with a woman named Lindsay."

"Visions?" Jennifer repeated, confusion evident in her voice. "Like dreams?"

"More real than a dream," Killian replied, shaking his head. "They feel like memories, but they don't make any sense. I love you and our family, Jen. I have no idea who this Lindsay person is or why I'm seeing this other life with her."

Jennifer's expression softened as she reached out to take his hand, intertwining their fingers. "That must be so confusing and frightening for you," she said gently. "I can't even imagine what that must feel like."

"Terrifying," Killian admitted, squeezing her hand. "And I don't know what to do about it. I don't want to make you or the kids worry, but these visions just won't go away."

"Killian," Jennifer said solemnly, her eyes locking with his, "I love you, and we'll get through this together. But we need to figure out what's causing these visions and how to stop them. I don't want our family to suffer because of something that isn't even real."

He could see the determination in her eyes, and for a moment, he felt reassured. But then, a dark cloud seemed to pass over her face, and she looked away, her grip on his hand tightening.

"Jen?" Killian asked hesitantly. "What's wrong?"

"Nothing," she replied quickly, forcing a smile. "I'm just worried, worried about you and what this could mean for us."

"Me too," Killian whispered, pulling her into a tight embrace. They stood there for a moment, their arms wrapped around each other, as the sun dipped below the horizon and darkness began to fall.

After dinner, Killian stood at the kitchen sink, scrubbing the grease from the frying pan, the soapy water building against his hands as he lost himself in the rhythmic motion. He tried to focus on the task before him, blocking out the intrusive visions of Lindsay that seemed to creep into his thoughts whenever his mind wandered.

"Hey, Dad!" Casey called out from the living room, pulling Killian back to reality. "Do you want to see a drawing I made?"

"Of course, buddy," Killian replied, rinsing the pan and setting it aside. He dried his hands on a towel and joined his son in the living room where he sat with colored pencils and drawing pad open before him. As he leaned down to look at Casey's drawing, the familiar scent of Jennifer's perfume wafted over him, grounding him in the present moment.

"All right, let's see what we have here," Killian said, pulling the drawing closer to him. As he looked at the picture, so proud of the detailed drawing and Casey's artistic ability, he said, "Wow Casey! This looks almost as good as a picture printed on the color printer." He kept his eyes fixed on Casey's eager face, determined not to let the specter of Lindsay distract him from being the father his children deserved.

"Thanks, Dad." Casey beamed when they finished. "You're the best!"

"Anytime, buddy." Killian ruffled his hair affectionately before standing up. "Now, go get ready for bed."

"Okay!" Casey scampered off toward his room, leaving Killian to survey the cozy domestic scene around him. Joe and Hannah were curled up on the couch, engrossed in their favorite cartoon, while Jennifer sat in her favorite side of the white linen couch, a well-worn copy of her favorite spiritual book resting on her lap.

"Everything okay?" Jennifer asked, her eyes searching Killian's face for any signs of distress.

"Everything's fine," Killian reassured her, forcing a smile. "Just looking at Casey's drawing."

"Good." Jennifer gave him a small nod of approval before turning back to her book. "Don't forget we have that PTA meeting tomorrow."

"Wouldn't dream of it," Killian replied, his voice steady despite the sudden flicker of Lindsay's face in his mind's eye.

Determined not to let the visions control him, Killian busied himself with tidying up the living room. He picked up scattered toys and folded discarded blankets all the while keeping up a steady stream of conversation with his Jennifer and the children. With each interaction, the image of Lindsay seemed to fade further into the background, replaced by the warmth and love of his family.

Later, as Killian tucked Joe and Hannah into bed, he felt a renewed sense of commitment to his life with Jennifer and their children. The visions may continue to haunt him, but he refused to let them consume his thoughts any longer. His family was his priority, and he resolved to be the best husband and father he could be, no matter what lingering shadows tried to pull him away from them.

"Good night, kiddos," Killian whispered, pressing a kiss to each of their foreheads. "I love you both so much."

"Love you too, Dad," they whispered sleepily, snuggling deeper into their covers.

With a final glance at their peaceful faces, Killian closed their doors softly behind him. As he made his way back to his bedroom, the ghostly figure of Lindsay stood waiting for him in the hallway, but this time, Killian walked past her without hesitation, his heart firmly in place with Jennifer and his beautiful family.

Chapter 3

Who Are You

Killian's hand trembled as he lifted the cup of coffee to his lips. The steam clouded over his face, and the rich aroma filled the air, momentarily distracting him from the turmoil brewing inside his mind. It had been happening more frequently over the past few weeks, the vivid visions that invaded his consciousness like an unwelcome guest, refusing to leave until they had completely consumed him.

"Everything okay?" Jennifer asked, her eyes filled with concern as she reached out to rest a gentle hand on his arm. Her touch was soft and comforting, but it couldn't erase the memories of another life that haunted him relentlessly.

"Uh, yeah," Killian replied, attempting to sound casual. He didn't want to worry her and remind her of the visions he has been having, but he couldn't deny the impact these visions were having on his life. As much as he tried to push them aside, they demanded his attention, growing in intensity and frequency.

"Are you sure? You've been so distant lately, and I can't help but worry."

"Really, Jen, I'm fine. Just tired, I guess," he lied, avoiding her gaze. He knew that if he looked into her eyes, he would see the love and loyalty she had always shown him. It made him feel guilty for longing for something he couldn't quite understand, the memories of a past life with Lindsay.

The visions had started as little more than fleeting images, easy enough to dismiss as mere daydreams. But as days turned into weeks, they began to take on a life of their own, pulling him deeper into a world he once shared with Lindsay, a world filled with laughter, adventure, and a passion that left him breathless.

"Promise me you'll tell me if something's wrong," Jennifer implored, her eyes searching his face for any sign of deception.

"Of course," Killian agreed, forcing a reassuring smile. But deep down, he knew that the time for hiding was drawing to an end. The visions had become too powerful, too real to ignore any longer.

As Jennifer turned her attention back to her phone, Killian's mind drifted once again to his past life with Lindsay. He could feel the warmth of her skin, hear the rhythm of her laughter, and see the spark in her eyes as they danced beneath the moonlit sky. It was as if he was reliving those moments all over again, a feeling that both excited and terrified him.

"Maybe you should take a break from work for a while," Jennifer suggested, her voice barely penetrating the haze of memories that enveloped him. "You know, get some rest, and clear your head."

"Maybe," Killian whispered absently, though he knew that rest would not be enough to quell the storm that raged within him. He couldn't ignore these visions any longer; they were affecting every aspect of his life, including his relationship with Jennifer.

The world he had shared with Lindsay was so different from the one he had built with Jennifer, leaving him torn between the present and the past. He found himself questioning his choices, his happiness, and, ultimately, the life he had chosen to live. But one thing was certain: he could no longer deny the truth that lay buried deep within him, waiting to be unearthed.

As the sun dipped below the horizon, casting long shadows across the room, Killian knew that he was standing at a crossroads. He could no longer pretend that everything was fine and that the memories of Lindsay were nothing more than figments of his imagination. The time had come to confront his fears and desires, even if it meant risking everything he held dear.

Killian's mind swirled with images of Lindsay, each more vivid and vibrant than the last. In his memories, she stood on the sun-soaked shoreline of a small coastal town in Carolina, her carefree laughter carried away by the soft ocean breeze. Her long sun-kissed hair danced around her face, framing her bright chestnut brown eyes that seemed to hold the secrets of the sea.

"Come on, Killian! The water's perfect," Lindsay called out, her voice as warm and inviting as the waves lapping against the shore. She was a free spirit, unafraid to chase her dreams and follow her heart wherever it led her. This sense of adventure had woven itself into the fabric of their relationship, as they explored both the world around them and the depths of their love for one another.

"All right, all right." Killian grinned, shaking off his hesitation and wading into the water to join her. Their hands intertwined, fingers laced together like the intricate patterns of a seashell, as they dove beneath the surface together, surrendering themselves to the powerful embrace of the ocean.

In contrast, his life with Jennifer felt routine and predictable, like a well-worn path that left no room for deviation or exploration. Their conversations were pleasant but lacked the sparkle and spontaneity that once flowed so freely between him and Lindsay. They spent their evenings watching television or discussing mundane details of their daily lives; such routine comfort paled in comparison to the exhilarating adventures he shared with Lindsay.

"Killian," Lindsay whispered one night as they lay entwined beneath a blanket of stars, "do you ever wonder if there's more to life than what we can see? Like maybe we're just tiny pieces of some grand cosmic puzzle?"

"Sometimes," Killian admitted, his thoughts drifting to the vast expanse of the universe above them. "But if I'm a piece of that puzzle, I'm glad I found the one that fits next to mine." He squeezed her hand gently, feeling both humbled and awed by the love that connected them.

"Me too," she whispered, her voice shaded with the same sense of wonderment that filled Killian's heart. It was in these quiet moments, when their souls seemed to intertwine like strands of moonlight, that Killian felt truly alive.

As his memories of Lindsay continued to play out behind his closed eyes, Killian couldn't help but compare the two lives he had lived. The one with Lindsay was a kaleidoscope of colors, each moment vivid and full of life; the other, with Jennifer, felt more like a grayscale painting, beautiful in its own right but lacking the vibrancy that once ignited his soul.

"Killian, are you all right?" Jennifer asked, her concern evident in her furrowed brow and tightly clasped hands. She had noticed the distant look in his eyes, the way he seemed to be living in another world entirely.

"I'm fine," he replied, forcing a smile onto his face even as his heart ached with longing for the life he had once shared with Lindsay. "Just lost in thought."

"Okay," Jennifer said, not entirely convinced but willing to let it go for now. "Just remember, I'm here if you need to talk."

"Thanks, Jen," Killian whispered, knowing that he would never be able to fully share the weight of his memories with her. For now, he would continue to navigate the murky waters of his past and present, hoping that somewhere within their depths, he might find the answers he so desperately sought.

The coastal town of Carolina shimmered like a mirage in Killian's memories, the salty air tickling his nose and the sound of seagulls cawing overhead. He could almost taste the fresh seafood they had feasted on time and time again—the succulent shrimp, buttery scallops, and flaky, melt-in-your-mouth fish. Colorful boats bobbed gently in the harbor, their sails full of wind and promise.

"Killian? Are you sure you're all right?" Jennifer asked, her voice pulling him back into the present moment.

"Y-yeah," he stammered, trying to focus on the reality before him but feeling the allure of his memories with Lindsay tugging at him like the tide. "Just remembering something."

"Something about our last vacation?" Jennifer questioned gently, attempting to share in the nostalgia that seemed to consume him.

"Uh, yeah. Something like that," Killian lied, feeling an overwhelming sense of guilt as he swam in the turbulent sea of his past with Lindsay and the tranquil pond of his life with Jennifer.

In his mind, he revisited sun-drenched days spent exploring hidden coves and quiet nights illuminated by the soft glow of bioluminescent algae. He remembered laughter shared over inside jokes, stolen kisses beneath the stars, and hands clasped together as they navigated the ever-changing landscape of their love.

"Jen, do you ever wonder if there's more to life than what we have now?" Killian found himself asking, his voice barely a whisper.

"Sometimes," she admitted, her eyes searching his face for clues to where his thoughts were wandering. "But I think we've built a good life together, Killian. Don't you?"

"Of course," he replied, his voice strained as the excitement of rediscovering his life with Lindsay warred with the terror of what it might mean for his life with Jennifer. "I just…I don't know."

"Killian, it's okay to reminisce about the past," Jennifer said gently, her eyes softening as she tried to bridge the gap between them. "But we can't live in our memories. We have to create new ones together."

"I know," he whispered, feeling the weight of his unspoken truth pressing down on him like a leaden anchor. Though he longed to share his heartache with Jennifer, he knew that some secrets were too dangerous to be revealed, secrets like the love he had once shared with Lindsay and the life he couldn't help but wonder if he had left behind.

"Let's go outside," Jennifer suggested, breaking through his daydream. "The sunset is supposed to be beautiful tonight."

"All right," Killian agreed, allowing her warm hand to guide him toward the door. As they stepped into the fading sunlight, he couldn't help but compare the muted hues of the sky to the vibrant sunsets he had once shared with Lindsay. But as he looked at Jennifer, her face aglow with the golden light, he realized that there was beauty in this life too, a different kind of beauty, born from the steady rhythms of a love built on trust and commitment.

"Isn't it amazing?" Jennifer asked, her voice filled with awe. "I've never seen anything quite like it."

"Neither have I," Killian whispered, his words carrying a double meaning that weighed heavily on his heart. As he watched the sun dip below the horizon, he knew he would have to find a way to reconcile his feelings for Lindsay with his commitment to Jennifer. Only then could he truly embrace the life he had chosen and the future that lay before him.

*****

Killian found himself drifting back to the memories of his past life with Lindsay, recalling their banter and conversations. As he stood on the porch with Jennifer, he couldn't help but contrast her gentle presence with the fiery energy that had once sparked between him and Lindsay.

"Hey there, stranger!" Lindsay's voice rang out in his mind, clear as day, as he remembered their first encounter at that beach party years ago. The wind had whipped her hair around her face, her eyes alight with laughter. "Care for a dance?"

"Only if you're ready to keep up," Killian had replied, smirking as he challenged her.

"Is that a challenge?" Lindsay had retorted, narrowing her eyes playfully.

"Maybe," Killian had said, their hands meeting for the first time.

As they danced under the starry sky, their laughter mingling with the crashing waves, Killian felt an undeniable connection. Long conversations about life and love followed, late into the night, until the sun began to rise, casting a warm glow over the sand.

"Wouldn't it be incredible to live our lives completely free?" Lindsay asked one night, her eyes reflecting the moonlight. "To follow our dreams without fear or hesitation?"

"Absolutely," Killian had agreed, his heart swelling with admiration for this woman who seemed to embody everything he had never known he wanted.

Their adventures continued, each seemingly more spectacular than the last. One of the most memorable was kayaking through a bioluminescent bay, the water glowing beneath them like a million stars, mirroring the sky above. Their laughter had echoed through the night, the magic of the moment etched forever in Killian's soul.

"Promise me we'll always have nights like these, Killian," Lindsay whispered, her hand finding his in the darkness.

"Always," he vowed, his heart aching with the weight of his promise.

*****

Back in the present, Killian blinked away his memories and focused on Jennifer's serene face bathed in the soft twilight. He knew he had to find a way to reconcile the passionate love he had once shared with Lindsay and the quiet, steady love that flowed between him and Jennifer. The journey to understanding his heart would be a difficult one, but it was a path he could no longer avoid.

Killian's restless gaze wandered to the window, where the sun dipped low in the sky, casting a gray, muted light over their small backyard. The once vibrant garden now seemed dull and lifeless, mirroring his own discontent. He could still feel the echo of Lindsay's laughter, the warmth of her hand in his, and the exhilaration of a life lived without boundaries.

"Killian?" Jennifer's voice cut through the silence, bringing him back to the moment. "Are you okay? You've been lost in thought all evening."

"Sorry," he mumbled, forcing a smile. "Just thinking about work. It's been…unfulfilling lately."

"Maybe you need a change," she suggested, reaching across the table to touch his hand. "You've been working at the same place for years. It might be time to try something new."

"Maybe," Killian agreed, but his thoughts were elsewhere. As Jennifer continued to discuss potential job opportunities, he couldn't help but compare the reality of his life with Jennifer to the vibrant memories of his life with Lindsay.

"Remember when we went on that weekend trip to the mountains?" Jennifer asked, smiling at the memory. "That was so much fun. We should do something like that again soon."

"Yeah, it was great," Killian replied, struggling to match her enthusiasm. The trip had been pleasant enough, but it paled in comparison to the wild adventures he'd experienced with Lindsay. His heart longed for the excitement of the open sea, the salty breeze that carried the promise of limitless possibilities. And yet here he sat, tethered to a life that offered only routine and predictability.

"Killian, are you even listening to me?" Jennifer's voice held a note of frustration as she withdrew her hand from his.

"Sorry, I didn't mean to drift off," he apologized, attempting to refocus on the conversation. "Who are we talking about?"

"Never mind." She sighed, disappointment etched in her features. "It's not important." She pushed her chair back and began clearing the dishes from the table.

Feeling a pang of guilt, Killian jumped up to help her. As they worked side by side, he couldn't shake the nagging feeling that he was missing something vital, that there was more to life than what he had with Jennifer. The vivid hues of his past with Lindsay stood in stark contrast to the monochrome existence that now seemed to surround him.

"Jen, do you ever wish we could just…escape?" he asked hesitantly, searching her face for understanding. "Like pack up our things and go on an adventure? Live our lives without fear or hesitation?"

"Maybe," she said, her voice shaded with doubt. "But we have responsibilities here. We can't just drop everything and run off whenever we feel like it."

Killian nodded but felt a hollow emptiness inside. He knew she was right; they were adults now, with steady jobs, a mortgage to pay, and children to protect and raise. And yet he couldn't shake the feeling that somewhere along the way, he'd lost a part of himself, the part that craved excitement, passion, and freedom.

As Killian lay in bed that night, he stared at the ceiling, unable to sleep. The memories of Lindsay continued to haunt him, stirring within him both longing and fear. He knew that he could no longer ignore the growing void between the life he once lived and the one he led now.

The following morning, Killian stood at the kitchen window, staring out at the small garden behind their house. The vibrant colors of Lindsay's world seemed to have seeped into his own, casting a new light on everything he saw. A sudden breeze rustled the wind chimes in the corner of the yard, and he was reminded of the chime-like laughter that had once filled his days with joy.

"Did you sleep well?" Jennifer asked as she entered the kitchen, her voice pulling him back to reality.

"Uh, yeah, I guess," he mumbled, still lost in the shifting landscape of his thoughts.

"Killian, what's going on? You've been distant lately," Jennifer said, concern etched in her face. "Is it something I did?"

He hesitated before answering, realizing this was the moment he needed to confront his feelings. Taking a deep breath, Killian began, "No, Jen, it's not you. It's just...I've been more of these dreams about my past...about Lindsay."

Jennifer looked puzzled but didn't interrupt. Killian continued, "We had this incredible life together, full of adventure and passion. And now, looking at our lives, I can't help but feel that we're missing out on something."

"Killian, are you saying—" Jennifer started, her voice shaky.

"Wait, let me finish," he interrupted, knowing he needed to get it all out. "These memories of Lindsay have made me realize that I want more for us, Jen, more than just routine and predictability. I want the excitement and the freedom we used to dream about when we first met."

"Are you suggesting we find that together, or are you saying you want to go back to her?" Jennifer asked, her eyes searching his for any hint of betrayal.

"Jen, I don't even know if going back to her is an option. But I do know that I want to live a more fulfilling life, and I want to do that with you," Killian admitted, his own vulnerability now exposed.

Jennifer's eyes softened, and she gave him a small smile. "I appreciate your honesty, Killian. Maybe it's time we made some changes in our lives."

"Really?" Killian asked, the anticipation of a new beginning igniting within him.

Chapter 4

Crawling from the Wreckage

Jennifer stood by the kitchen window, her shoulder-length curly brown hair catching the morning light as it streamed through the lace curtains. Her sharp hazel eyes scanned the garden outside, observing every detail with a protective intensity that had become second nature to her over the years.

"Jen," Killian called from the bedroom, "have you seen my tie?"

"Third drawer on the left, darling," she replied without hesitation, her voice carrying the same strength as her gaze.

Jennifer moved gracefully about the kitchen, the sun casting a warm glow on her elegant features. She possessed a natural, undeniable beauty that went far beyond physical appearance; it was an aura that radiated warmth and kindness. Her strong-willed demeanor often masked this inner beauty, but those who truly knew Jennifer could see it shining through her every action.

As she prepared breakfast for her family, Jennifer's thoughts drifted to the people she loved most in the world: her husband, their children, and her dear friends. She pondered the trials they had faced together and how their love for each other had been the glue that held them all together during even the most difficult times. It was this unyielding love that made Jennifer's heart swell with pride and gratitude, knowing that she was surrounded by such unwavering support and affection.

"Here it is!" Killian exclaimed from the bedroom, having found his tie at last. He entered the kitchen, adjusting the knot as he approached Jennifer. "You always know where everything is," he said, looking up at her with admiration.

"Years of practice," she replied, offering him a warm smile as she placed a plate of eggs and toast before him.

"Thank you, my love," Killian said, leaning in to give her a tender kiss on the cheek.

Jennifer's hazel eyes sparkled with affection as she watched him sit down to eat. She knew that no matter what challenges lay ahead, the love she shared with her family would be there to guide and support them all and as long as they had that love, they could face anything together.

"All right, I'm off to work," Killian announced, standing up from the table after finishing his breakfast. He grabbed his briefcase and keys and kissed Jennifer once more before making his way toward the front door.

"Drive safe," she called after him, still standing by the kitchen window, her eyes following him as he climbed into his black Audi sports car.

"Come on, baby," he whispered affectionately to the car as he turned the key, listening with satisfaction as the engine roared to life. It was an affirmation that despite the rough patches he had experienced lately, there were still things in life that brought him joy.

As he drove through the rain-soaked city streets, weaving effortlessly through the light traffic, the radio blared country tunes that seemed to harmonize perfectly with the morning's ambiance. He hummed along, lost in thought about the presentation he was due to deliver later that day and how it could potentially boost his career.

"Today is going to be a good day," Killian muttered, tapping his fingers rhythmically on the steering wheel. His anticipation for success surged within him, like a steady current of energy. He could already envision Jennifer's proud smile when he'd tell her how well everything went.

The autumn sun slid behind a storm cloud, casting a chilling breeze across Jennifer's face as she sat in the rocking chair on their porch. The scent of rain hung in the air, and the first drops began to fall, softly tapping against the windows. She pulled her shawl tighter around her shoulders and thought back over the years she had been with Killian.

"Mom, do you remember when Dad took us camping?" Their daughter, Hannah, asked from the doorway, holding a photo album in her hands.

Jennifer smiled warmly at the memory. "Oh, I do. Although your father had his share of camping when he was your age, he was determined to share with you kids the same experiences he was fortunate to have as a kid."

"Say what you will about that trip," Hannah chuckled, "but it taught me how to build a fire in the pouring rain."

"Your father has always been one for teaching by his examples," Jennifer replied, her eyes filled with quiet admiration. "He's given us a life full of love and security, and I couldn't ask for anything more."

"Neither could we, Mom," Hannah agreed, sitting down beside her mother on the porch steps.

Jennifer turned her gaze toward the distant skyscrapers, her thoughts shifting to the challenges they had faced together: the numerous job changes, the financial struggles, and even the heartbreaking loss of loved ones. Through it all, Jennifer's loyalty to her family had never wavered, providing them with unwavering support and comfort.

"Mrs. Flaherty, I'd like to talk to you about the recent developments in the neighborhood," said Mr. Jefferson, their neighbor, approaching the porch hesitantly.

"Of course," Jennifer replied, eyeing him cautiously. She was slow to trust others when faced with unexpected challenges, having learned to rely on her instincts to protect her family.

"Several families are considering selling their properties," he explained. "A developer is offering quite a substantial sum, and many are tempted by the promise of a fresh start."

Jennifer furrowed her brow, considering the implications. She knew that selling their home would uproot their lives, potentially causing more harm than good.

"Thank you for letting us know," she responded diplomatically, carefully masking her concern. "I will call Killian on his cellphone now to make him aware of this."

"Please do," Mr. Jefferson nodded. "Some of us are meeting at my house tomorrow to discuss our options further. You're welcome to join us."

"Thank you," Jennifer said, watching him walk away. As the rain began to fall harder, she felt a surge of determination well up within her. She was not afraid to make tough decisions and fight for what she believed in. And she would do whatever it took to keep her family's best interests at heart.

"Mom, are we going to sell our home?" Hannah asked, an anxious tremble in her voice.

"I will call your dad now, but let's wait for your father to come home before we discuss this more," Jennifer replied softly, her arm wrapping protectively around her daughter. "We'll all talk about it together.

But know this, Hannah, no matter what decision we make, it will always be with our family's happiness in mind."

"Okay," Hannah whispered, leaning against her mother as they watched the rain fall steadily, knowing that they could weather any storm as long as they had each other.

*****

After chatting with Jennifer on the phone, Killian's fingers drummed lightly on the leather steering wheel, a rhythmic tapping that mirrored the pattering raindrops against the windshield of his black Audi sports car. The wipers swept back and forth, clearing the way for him to navigate through the slick streets as he drove toward his office.

"Stay safe out there, drivers," the radio announcer warned. "This downpour is expected to continue throughout the day."

"Great," Killian muttered under his breath, his warm smile concealed beneath the furrow of his brow. He cast a glance toward the clock on the dashboard, noting the time with a sigh. There was still much to do at the office, but his thoughts were tethered to Jennifer and their conversation he just had with her on the phone.

"Killian, I just wanted to let you know that Mr. Jefferson told me about the rezoning plans today," Jennifer had said over the phone, her voice steady but shaded with worry. "He says some of the neighbors are considering selling their homes before it affects property values."

"Let's not jump to conclusions," Killian replied, the practical thinker in him attempting to remain calm. "We'll discuss it tonight, all right?"

"Of course, my love," she responded, her loyalty and support shining through even amidst uncertainty.

The red stoplight cast a crimson glow upon Killian's face as he came to a halt, allowing his mind to wander back to his wife. He knew Jennifer would be cautious in trusting others when faced with unexpected challenges like this, yet he also knew she was strong-willed and unafraid to fight for what she believed in. It was one of the many reasons he loved her so dearly.

As the light turned green, Killian pressed on the accelerator, feeling the powerful engine respond smoothly beneath him. A sense of unease gnawed at his chest, making it difficult to concentrate on the road ahead. He couldn't shake the feeling that their lives were about to change drastically, and not necessarily for the better.

"Jennifer," he whispered to himself, seeking solace in her name. "We'll figure this out together."

The rain continued its relentless assault against the car, each droplet echoing Killian's growing concerns for his family's future. But as he drove onward, he knew deep down that they would face whatever challenges lay ahead with unwavering determination and love. For it was in moments like these that he was reminded of the strength of their bond, a connection that could weather any storm.

At the next intersection, Killian slowed to a stop, waiting for the traffic light to change. The seconds ticked by, each one stretching out like an eternity. A bead of sweat trickled down his temple, a stark reminder of the pressure resting on his shoulders.

"Come on, come on," he urged the red light, his grip tightening on the wheel. He needed this win, not just for himself but for Jennifer too. They had been trying to reignite their passion, and a victory today would surely help boost their spirits.

The moment the light turned green, Killian pressed down on the accelerator, eager to leave his worries behind in a cloud of exhaust. As his car sped forward, he felt invincible, as if the world was finally bending to his will.

That feeling shattered in an instant.

Through the blur of motion, Killian caught sight of another car, speeding toward him from the side. Its horn blared, a desperate cry that pierced through the music and his thoughts. Panic surged like ice water through his veins.

"No!" he shouted, swerving desperately to avoid the impending collision. But it was too late. The sickening crunch of metal against metal echoed through the air as the two vehicles collided, the impact hurling Killian's sports car into a wild spin.

As the world around him spun into chaos, Killian's mind raced with frantic thoughts. His heart pounded in his chest, a drumbeat that seemed to harmonize with the rapid-fire images flashing before his eyes—moments shared with Jennifer, dreams of their future together, and the life he had built for himself.

And then, everything went dark.

Unbeknownst to Killian, as his body slumped over the steering wheel, unconscious and trapped within the twisted wreckage of his beloved sports car, the cruel hands of fate were weaving a new thread into the tapestry of his life. The coma that now gripped him would become both a prison and a gateway, leading him down a path of love, loss, and heartache that he could never have predicted.

*****

The shrill ringing of the telephone pierced through the quiet morning air, echoing off the walls of the small, cozy living room. Jennifer hurried to answer it, her heart pounding in her chest as an inexplicable sense of dread washed over her. As she pressed the receiver to her ear, her hand trembled ever so slightly.

"Hello?" she whispered, her voice barely audible.

"Mrs. Flaherty? This is Dr. Stevens from St. Mary's Hospital."

Jennifer's heart skipped a beat, and she felt her knees buckle beneath her weight. She steadied herself against the wall, her other hand gripping the phone with white knuckles.

"Wh-what's wrong?" She managed to choke out, desperately trying to quell the rising panic within her.

"Your husband, Killian, has been in a car accident. He's in a coma. I'm so sorry," the voice on the other end said, filled with genuine sympathy.

A guttural wail tore itself from Jennifer's throat, filling the room with a terrible sound that seemed to echo her own shattered heart. Her children rushed to her side, their faces etched with concern. Casey took the phone from her trembling hand, listening intently as Dr. Stevens relayed the devastating news.

Casey could only stand there in stunned silence, the words *coma* and *accident* swirling around him like a tornado. He tried to speak, to comfort his mother, but no words came. Instead, he wrapped his arms around her, holding her close as her body wracked with sobs.

*****

Jennifer stood alone in the hospital chapel, a sanctuary of calm amid the storm of emotions raging inside her. The hushed whispers of prayer and the faint scent of burning candles enveloped her, offering a small measure of solace in her darkest hour. Her hands clenched into fists, knuckles white as she fought to hold onto her faith.

"God," she whispered, her voice trembling with emotion. "Please…please don't take him away from us."

Tears streamed down her cheeks, leaving a trail of anguish in their wake. She knew Killian was strong, but even the strongest people sometimes faltered in the face of adversity. Jennifer's heart ached at the thought of losing him, of a life without his laughter, his love, and his unwavering support.

"Give him strength," she begged, her words barely audible. "Give him the will to fight."

As she stood there, praying for a miracle, Jennifer couldn't help but feel the weight of uncertainty pressing down upon her. The future stretched out before her like a vast ocean, dark and unfathomable, filled with both hope and despair. And as she stared into its depths, she found herself clinging to her faith, her love for Killian the only beacon of light in the darkness that threatened to consume her.

*****

In the sterile hospital room, Killian lay motionless, a ghostly figure bathed in the dim glow of the monitors that surrounded him. The machines beeped and whirred tirelessly as they breathed for him, pumped his blood, and kept vigil over his fragile existence. His once vibrant eyes were hidden beneath closed lids, shrouding the world from their piercing gaze.

"Killian," a voice whispered softly in his mind, gentle as a summer breeze.

Suddenly, he found himself transported back to the quaint coastal town in Carolina, his senses alive with the memories of a life long forgotten. Killian's vision grew sharper, his surroundings taking form, a cozy restaurant filled with the warmth of laughter and the clink of glasses raised in celebration. Seated across from him was Lindsay, her eyes sparkling with mischief as she playfully stole a piece of dessert from his plate.

"Hey!" He feigned indignation, unable to suppress the grin that spread across his face. "That was mine!"

"Finders keepers." She laughed, her tongue darting out to catch a stray droplet of chocolate sauce. "Besides, you know you love me too much to be mad."

"Guilty as charged," he admitted, reaching across the table to take her hand. The feel of her skin against his sent a shiver down his spine, a sensation both familiar and foreign. A pang of longing resonated deep within him.

"Remember our wedding day?" Lindsay asked, her voice laced with nostalgia.

The restaurant faded away, replaced by the delicate beauty of an outdoor ceremony. Sunlight filtered through the trees, casting shadows on the guests who had gathered to bear witness to their union. Killian stood at the altar, heart pounding in anticipation as he watched Lindsay make her way toward him, radiant in her flowing white gown.

"From this moment," he vowed, gazing into her eyes as he slipped a ring onto her finger, "I promise to love and cherish you for all the days of my life."

"Until death do us part," Lindsay echoed, tears glistening in her eyes. Their lips met in a tender, soul-searing kiss, sealing their commitment to one another before the world.

As the memory faded, Killian found himself once again ensnared by the cold embrace of the hospital bed. The images of his past life with Lindsay flickered through his mind like a reel of a forgotten film, leaving him disoriented and craving more. His heart ached for the woman who had filled his life with laughter and love, a longing that threatened to tear him apart from within.

"Where are you now, Lindsay?" he wondered silently, lost amidst the tangled threads of his fractured memories.

During the swirling mists that veiled his comatose mind, Killian wandered through a sunlit meadow, the air rich with the scent of wildflowers. Lindsay danced ahead of him, her laughter tinkling like silver bells as she wove daisy chains and threaded them into her hair. She was the epitome of carefree joy, and Killian found himself drawn to her like a moth to a flame.

"Come on, Killian!" she called, tossing her head back, the sunlight catching in her golden tresses. "Let's walk by the river."

Her hand slipped into his, and Killian marveled at the warmth of her touch, so tangible that it felt as if she were truly there with him. As they strolled along the water's edge, their fingers entwined, Killian felt a deep-seated connection to this woman who had once been his everything.

"Remember how we used to spend our days here?" Lindsay asked, her voice soft and tender. "We were inseparable, like two halves of a whole."

Killian nodded, his heart swelling with affection as he recalled those days. Yet even as he reveled in the memories, a shadow of guilt crept into the corners of his mind. For though his heart belonged to Lindsay in these visions, it was Jennifer who held it in reality.

"Jen…" he whispered, the name slipping from his lips without conscious thought. The weight of his conflicting emotions settled heavily within him, threatening to crush him beneath its crushing presence.

"Who's Jen?" Lindsay questioned, her eyes narrowing.

"Jennifer…she's my—" Killian faltered, unable to find the words that would do justice to the complicated web of feelings that ensnared him.

"Your what?" Lindsay pressed, her playful demeanor replaced by something colder, more distant.

"Jennifer is…I love her," he admitted, the truth striking him like a bolt of lightning. "But I loved you too, once upon a time."

"Once upon a time?" Lindsay echoed, her voice laced with bitterness. "Is that all our love has become to you—a fairy tale?"

"Of course not!" Killian insisted, his heart twisting in agony. "I cherish the memories we shared, and I always will. But my life now…it's with Jennifer. I can't just abandon her."

"Then what do you want, Killian?" Lindsay demanded, tears pooling in her eyes as she gripped his hand tightly. "Why are you here with me, when your heart belongs to someone else?"

"I don't know." He confessed, his voice barely a whisper. The pain of his dilemma bore down on him like an unrelenting storm, leaving him battered and broken in its wake.

As the day dissolved around him, Killian felt himself sinking deeper into the murky depths of uncertainty, torn between the love of two women who both held claim to his heart.

*****

In the sterile hospital room, Killian lay motionless on the cold bed, his chest rising and falling in sync with the rhythmic beeping of the machines that surrounded him. The persistent hum of fluorescent lights above cast unnatural shadows across his pale face. The sharp smell of antiseptic hung heavy in the air, mingling with the faint scent of despair that seemed to cling to every surface.

"Damn it, Killian, you always have to be the center of attention," muttered Catherine, his sister, her eyes red-rimmed and her fists clenched at her sides. Her voice was brittle, a thin veneer of anger masking the raw pain beneath.

"Catherine!" Their father chastised, though he could not hide the tremor in his own voice.

"Sorry, Dad...I just can't believe this is happening." Catherine turned away, struggling to maintain her composure.

Killian's best friend, Brian, stood at the foot of the bed, staring down at his unconscious friend with an expression of utter despair. "I should've been there for him," he whispered, his voice cracking as he fought back tears. "Maybe if I had, he wouldn't be here like this."

"Brian, don't do that to yourself," Killian's mother said softly, her tear-streaked face a testament to her own heartache. "You know Killian wouldn't want you blaming yourself."

"Doesn't make it any easier," Brian replied, unable to meet her gaze.

As Killian's family and friends huddled together in the cramped room, a sense of overwhelming helplessness settled over them like a shroud. Unable to speak or move, Killian remained trapped within his own mind, each vision of Lindsay pulling him further away from the life he had built with Jennifer. He longed to reach out to them, to reassure them that he was still there, still fighting to find his way back. But the gulf between his consciousness and the world outside seemed insurmountable.

"Killian," his mother whispered, her hand trembling as she reached out to brush a lock of hair from his forehead. "Please, come back to us."

Her voice echoed through the void that separated them, like a faint beacon of light in the darkness. And in that moment, Killian knew that he could not give up—not while those he loved were left to suffer in his absence.

"Please, Killian," Catherine whispered, her anger giving way to desperation. "We need you."

"Stay strong, buddy," Brian implored, his voice heavy with emotion. "You've never backed down from a fight before."

As their words washed over him, Killian clung to the love that bound them together—the one constant in a world that seemed to be slipping further and further away. Determined to bridge the chasm that threatened to consume him, he focused on the familiar hum of the fluorescent lights, the sharp scent of antiseptic, and the sound of his family's voices as they prayed for his recovery.

And somewhere, deep within the recesses of his mind, a flicker of hope began to burn.

The fluorescent lights cast a sterile glow on the room as Jennifer entered, her heart heavy with anticipation. She hated hospitals—the way they smelled of antiseptic and death and the way they seemed to swallow time and hope in equal measure. But she had come here for Killian, to see him through this ordeal even if it meant facing her own fears.

"Killian," she whispered, drawing closer to his bedside. His chest rose and fell with each mechanical breath, the beeping and whirring of the machines a constant reminder of how precarious his condition was. As she looked at him, lying there so lifeless and vulnerable, she could not help but think of the dreams that had begun to haunt her—dreams of another woman who seemed to hold a piece of Killian's heart that Jennifer had never known existed.

"Who is she?" Jennifer demanded, her voice trembling with anger and jealousy. "Who is this Lindsay you keep dreaming about?"

In his coma, Killian remained oblivious to her turmoil. He was lost in another world, one where he and Lindsay danced beneath the stars and exchanged vows on a windswept beach. The memories were so vivid, the emotions so raw, that he could almost feel the warmth of her touch and hear the sound of her laughter.

"Jennifer," Killian whispered in his sleep, his voice distant and shaded with longing. "I'm sorry…I just can't forget her."

"Can't forget her?" Jennifer snapped, her hands clenching into fists at her sides. "You're supposed to be in love with me, Killian, not some ghost from your past!"

Tears streamed down her face, tracing hot trails of anguish that seemed to scorch her very soul. She wanted to scream, to rage against the injustice of it all, but she knew that it would do no good. All she could do was watch as the man she loved slipped further and further away, caught in the grip of a love that seemed to transcend even the boundaries of life itself.

"Please, Killian," she pleaded, her voice breaking. "Wake up. Come back to me."

But the silence that answered her was deafening, an abyss that seemed to grow wider with each passing moment. As she stood there, watching him drift between worlds, Jennifer could not help but wonder if this was the end—if Killian would ever wake from his coma or if he would remain trapped in his dreams of Lindsay forever.

"Killian," she whispered one last time, her voice barely audible amidst the hum of the fluorescent lights. "Please don't leave us."

As the uncertainty of what lay ahead settled over her like a shroud, Jennifer took a deep breath, steeling herself for whatever fate had in store. She knew that nothing was certain—not Killian's recovery, nor the future they had once dreamed of together. But she also knew that she would not give up on him, not without a fight.

"Stay with us, Killian," she whispered, her voice a mix of hope and heartache. "We need you now more than ever."

Chapter 5

Should I Stay or Should I Go

Killian's firstborn son Casey was the kind of person who could walk into a room and set it alight with his mere presence. He had a knack for making everyone around him feel like they were part of something truly special; his laughter was contagious, his smile warm, and his energy boundless. With his well-manicured chestnut hair and twinkling brown eyes, Casey exuded an aura that seemed to say, "Life is a party, and I'm here to make sure you enjoy every moment."

While most people might have been crushed under the weight of having their father in a coma, Casey chose to face this difficult situation with his unique brand of humor. He would often crack jokes about how much sleep his dad must be getting or how he had always wanted to learn ventriloquism so that he could have one-sided conversations with him. It was his way of dealing with the pain, and it seemed to work not only for himself but also for those around him.

"Hey, Joe, did you know that Dad is now officially the world-record holder for the longest nap?" Casey quipped to his brother one day as they stood by Killian's bedside. "I bet he'll wake up ready to throw one of his rum punch pool parties!"

Joe shook his head, trying to suppress a smile. "You are unbelievable, Casey," he said. "How can you keep joking at a time like this?"

Casey leaned against the hospital bed rail, his eyes fixed on his father's motionless form. "What else am I supposed to do?" he asked, his voice softening. "It's not like Dad's going to wake up just because we're all moping around feeling sorry for ourselves. We've got to stay strong for him, right? And if making people laugh helps them forget their worries for a little while, then I think that's worth doing."

As the brothers continued their conversation, Casey couldn't help but notice the way his dad's face had changed since he'd been in the coma. Though still bearing a strong resemblance to the man they knew and loved, Killian's features were now marked by lines of worry and exhaustion, a testament to the toll that the coma was taking on him.

"Besides," Casey added, "I like to think that if Dad could hear us right now, he'd want us to stay positive and keep our spirits up. You know how much he hates seeing us upset."

In those moments, when Casey filled the sterile hospital room with laughter, it felt almost as if his father were still with them, watching over them as they navigated this difficult period in their lives. And though the future remained uncertain, one thing was clear: Casey would continue to use his humor to bring light to even the darkest of situations, just as his father had taught him to do.

In contrast to Casey's exuberant spirit, Joe seemed like a quiet river running through the chaotic world around him. He was tall and lean, with curly blonde hair that fell into his deep-set eyes, which were always observing, always taking in more than they let on. He had a wisdom well beyond his years, as if he carried the weight of ancient knowledge within him.

"Hey, Casey," Joe spoke softly, a gentle smile playing on his lips. "Why don't you go grab us some coffee from the cafeteria? I think we could all use a break."

"Sure thing, bro." Casey nodded before leaving the room, his laughter echoing down the hallway.

As soon as the door clicked shut behind him, Joe crossed the room to stand by his father's bedside. The beeping monitors and soft hums of medical equipment filled the silence as Joe took Killian's hand, holding it carefully between his own.

"Hey, Dad," he whispered, his voice barely audible. "It's me, Joe. I'm here for you, all right?"

Though he knew his father couldn't hear him, Joe felt comforted by the familiar warmth of Killian's skin against his own. He closed his eyes, allowing himself a moment of vulnerability as he tried to send strength through their connected hands.

"Your energy is healing, Joe," his mother often told him. "You have a gift, a way of calming storms both inside and out."

And indeed, Joe's presence was like a balm to those around him, especially now. As he stood in the sterile hospital room, he drew upon the knowledge that seemed to flow through him like a river, steadying himself and nurturing the hope that his father would one day awaken.

"It's tough, you know?" He confided, opening his eyes again. "Casey's doing his best to keep our spirits up, but I can tell he's hurting too. We all are."

He paused, taking a deep breath before continuing. "But I won't let this break us, Dad. I'll take care of Mom and the others, just like you would've wanted. We'll get through this together, as a family."

As Joe spoke, it was as if a soothing energy filled the room, chasing away the shadows of fear and doubt. Though his father lay still in the coma, there was a sense of peace that seemed to emanate from Joe, wrapping itself around everyone in its gentle embrace.

"Stay strong, Dad," he whispered, his voice full of determination. "We're waiting for you, so don't give up on us now."

In that moment, Joe knew that his purpose went beyond what any school could teach him. He would be the calm amidst the storm, the guiding light in times of darkness. And if he had faith in himself and the ones he loved, they would face whatever challenges life threw at them with unwavering strength and courage.

Hannah stood in the doorway of the hospital room, her heart heavy with worry. The fading sunlight cast a golden glow upon her face, highlighting the delicate contours that made her the spitting image of her mother. Her eyes, however, pools of liquid warmth trapped between storm clouds of concern, were undeniably her father's.

"Hey, sis," Joe said softly, breaking the silence. "How are you holding up?"

Hannah blinked away the tears threatening to spill from her eyes and offered him a weak smile. Her chest tightened as she thought of her father lying there, pale and unresponsive. "I'm…I don't know, Joe," she admitted, her voice barely above a whisper. "It's just so hard to see him like this."

Joe rose from his chair and wrapped an arm around her shoulders, gently steering her into the room. As they approached their father's bedside, Hannah's fingers trembled, her instinct to protect those she loved warring with the fear that had settled deep within her bones.

"Sit down, Hannah." Joe guided her to the chair he had just vacated, his calm demeanor soothing her frayed nerves. "You don't have to be strong all the time, you know. We're here for each other."

In the quiet moments that followed, Hannah allowed herself to give in to the emotions she had been suppressing, her tears finally escaping their prison.

She stared at her father's still form, her thoughts a storm of memories and unspoken fears.

"Joe, what if…what if he never wakes up?" The words caught in her throat, raw and painful. "I can't bear the thought of losing him."

"Neither can I," Joe replied, his own voice laced with emotion. He squeezed her hand reassuringly. "But we can't let our fear consume us, Hannah. Dad wouldn't want that. We have to keep believing that he'll come back to us."

Hannah nodded, her gaze never leaving their father. She drew in a shuddering breath, trying to dispel the shadows that had taken root in her heart. "You're right," she whispered. "It's just so hard."

"Of course it is." Joe's gentle smile was both understanding and encouraging. "But remember, you don't have to face this alone. Casey, Mom, and I, we're all here for you."

In that moment, surrounded by the unwavering support of her family, Hannah began to feel the crushing weight of her fears lessen. It was as if Joe's steadfast presence had chased away some of the darkness, illuminating a path forward through the storm.

"Thank you, Joe," she whispered, her voice thick with gratitude. "I don't know what I would do without you."

"Let's hope we never have to find out," he said softly, his eyes reflecting the fierce determination that burned within them all. "We're in this together, Hannah. No matter what happens, we'll face it as a family."

With that promise tucked securely in her heart, Hannah knew they would find the strength to endure, not only for their father but also for each other. And though the future remained uncertain, one thing was clear: they would navigate its treacherous waters hand in hand, their love for one another an unbreakable anchor amidst the storm.

The hospital room was bathed in a soft, otherworldly glow. It was a quiet sanctuary where time seemed to slow down, its merciless march momentarily halted by the steady beep of the heart monitor. In the center of it all, Killian lay motionless, his face pale and etched with lines that spoke of a life well-lived.

Jennifer sat at her husband's bedside, her eyes tracing every contour of his face, memorizing each wrinkle as if they were sacred text. Her fingers, trembling ever so slightly, reached out to brush a few strands of graying hair from his forehead, the coolness of his skin sending a shiver down her spine. How she longed to see those familiar hazel eyes open once more, to feel the warmth of his smile as he teased her about something inconsequential.

"Killian," she whispered, her voice barely audible above the hum of the machines keeping him tethered to this world. "I don't know if you can hear me, but I need you to fight, my love. Our children…they need you too." The words caught in her throat, tears threatening to spill over as she clung to the tenuous thread of hope that bound them together.

She leaned in closer, her breath brushing against his ear like a lover's secret. "Do you remember when we first met, Killian? You were so sure of yourself, so confident in your pursuit. You always said you'd never give up on me, and you didn't." Jennifer allowed herself a small bittersweet smile, recalling the way he had relentlessly pursued her until she finally agreed to that first date, a decision that had changed the course of both their lives.

"Please, don't give up now. I know things have been…difficult lately, but we'll get through this. Together." As the dam of her emotions threatened to burst, Jennifer closed her eyes and sent a silent prayer into the void, hoping against hope that her words would somehow reach him.

"Remember our vows, Killian? For better or for worse…in sickness and in health. I meant every word, and I know you did too. You're not just my husband…you're my best friend, my rock. You've always been there for me, even when I didn't realize it."

Taking a deep, steadying breath, Jennifer opened her eyes and looked down at her husband's motionless form. "So now, I need you to fight, Killian. Fight for us, for Casey, Joe, Hannah, and me. We're here, by your side, ready to face whatever comes our way. But we need you with us, love."

The words hung in the air, heavy with promise and longing, their echoes lingering long after they had been spoken. And as Jennifer sat there, watching over the man who had been her partner through life's triumphs and tribulations, she couldn't help but feel that somewhere, deep within the recesses of his unconscious mind, Killian was listening and fighting with all the strength he could muster, for the family who loved him so fiercely.

*****

The beep of the heart monitor filled the room, a room that had become Killian's world. He lay motionless, suspended between life and death in a coma following a catastrophic car accident. His once chiseled features were now softened by the pallor of his unshaven face. Killian's body remained anchored to the hospital bed, but his mind drifted, wandering through the maze of memories that swirled around him.

"Killian, can you hear me?" The spectral voice of Jennifer, his wife, filtered through the haze. She was part of his present, a constant presence at his bedside, even though he could not see her.

"Jennifer," Killian whispered, his voice choked with emotion. But she couldn't hear him. No one could.

"Please come back to us," Jennifer pleaded, her hands clutching his limply. Those hands that had held so many memories: laughter, tears, triumphs, and defeats. They were intertwined with their beautiful children and the life they had built together.

"Come on, Killian. Don't give up on us." Her words peppered his thoughts like raindrops, each one piercing his consciousness.

But another voice called out to him, one from his past, like a siren's song beckoning him to follow. It was Lindsay, his first love, the woman who had occupied his dreams before Jennifer.

"Killian, do you remember the time we chased fireflies through the meadow? And how we used to dance beneath the stars?" The warmth of Lindsay's voice washed over him, and he felt his heart ache with longing for the simpler, happier times they had shared.

"Of course, I remember," he whispered, feeling foolish for talking to a memory but compelled by its pull. "I've just been…busy."

"Busy living the life you chose," Lindsay replied softly, a hint of sadness in her voice. "But it's not too late, Killian."

Killian hesitated, torn between the life he had with Jennifer and the memories of blissful days spent with Lindsay. The two women—one the anchor of his present and the other a ghost from his past—both held pieces of his heart.

"Please, Killian…come back to us," Jennifer implored, her voice heavy with tears. Her words stung him with guilt. How could he entertain thoughts of Lindsay when his wife and children needed him so desperately?

"Remember our love, Killian. It was pure, untainted by the burdens of this world," Lindsay whispered, her voice a balm against the harsh reality of his situation.

"Jen...I'm sorry." Killian choked out, trying to force himself back into his body, willing himself to wake up and be the man she needed him to be. But the fragments of his past life with Lindsay glowed like embers, refusing to be extinguished.

"Killian, don't forget me. Our love is still alive, waiting for you," Lindsay urged gently, tugging at his heartstrings, reminding him of all they had once shared.

"Killian, dear, we're still here, loving you. We will always love you. Please come back." Jennifer sobbed, her words a lifeline in the tumultuous sea of his emotions.

"Jen...Lindsay..." Killian stammered, feeling the weight of both lives bearing down upon him, pulling him in opposite directions. He longed to find solace in the arms of either woman but knew that no matter what path he chose, he would forever be haunted by the one he left behind.

Killian's heart raced as the visions of his past with Lindsay blurred with the present reality of Jennifer and their children, leaving him feeling trapped in a vortex of emotions. The sterile scent of the hospital room and the rhythmic beeping of machines filled his senses, grounding him in a world he could no longer touch.

"Killian, don't you see what these visions mean? You're here with me now, and our family is everything we've built together," Jennifer's voice whispered in his ear, her words like daggers stabbing at his heart. He could almost feel her warm breath against his skin, but it never quite reached him.

"Jen, I..." Killian's thoughts trailed off, his fear palpable as he grappled with the implications of his visions. Was he betraying his life with Jennifer by entertaining memories of Lindsay? What if he couldn't shake the ghost of his past, even after waking up? Would his love for Jennifer crumble under the weight of his longing for Lindsay?

"Killian, don't fight what your heart desires. Embrace our love, and let it guide you back to me," Lindsay urged, her voice softer, like silk brushing against his soul.

"Enough!" Killian cried out, clenching his fists in a desperate attempt to suppress the conflicting emotions that threatened to tear him apart. He had to find a way to protect his life with Jennifer and their children from the seductive allure of his past with Lindsay.

*****

"I'm sorry to interrupt, but I need to discuss something with you regarding your husband's condition." A new voice intruded upon Killian's turmoil. It was Dr. Jeffrey Cohen, the chief neurologist at St. Mary's Hospital and a coma specialist in the medical field. "I understand how difficult this has been for you, but we must consider all options, including the possibility of removing Killian's life support."

Jennifer's breath hitched, her eyes brimming with tears as she stared at Dr. Cohen, his words a cold reminder of the harsh reality they faced. Killian could feel her anguish reverberating through their connection, and it filled him with dread.

"Dr. Cohen, I—" Jennifer choked as she looked down at Killian's lifeless form, her hands trembling. "I need more time to think about it. I just can't—"

"Of course, Mrs. Flaherty," Dr. Cohen replied, his voice gentle but firm. "But we cannot wait indefinitely. We must make a decision in the best interest of your husband and your family. I will set up an appointment for you and I to discuss all the options in more detail."

*****

Killian's heart clenched, his fear mutating into terror as he realized the gravity of the situation. He had to find a way to break free from the prison of his own mind or risk losing everything he held dear, his wife, his children, and the life they'd built together. But he couldn't ignore the siren call of Lindsay's love, which seemed to wrap itself around him like a coil of smoke, haunting his every thought.

The room was bathed in a muted, golden light as the setting sun filtered through the blinds. The long shadows cast by the furniture seemed to mirror the dark thoughts that consumed Killian's mind. He lay there, trapped within his body, while Jennifer sat beside him, her fingers nervously tapping on the armrest of the chair.

"Killian," she whispered, tears shimmering in her eyes as she tried to reach him. "I don't know what to do."

He could feel her pain, a tangible thing that weighed heavy in the air between them. And yet he couldn't get rid of the doubt that gnawed at his heart, the visions of Lindsay that beckoned to him like a siren's call. It was as if an invisible wall had been erected between them, built from their unspoken fears and regrets.

"Can you hear me?" Jennifer asked, her voice cracking under the strain of her emotions. "Please just give me a sign that you're still in there…that you're still fighting."

Killian's soul ached to respond, to wrap her in his arms, and to assure her that everything would be okay. But the words remained trapped inside him, silenced by the relentless tide of memories that threatened to drown him.

"Is this really the life we were meant to have?" He wondered, tormented by the visions of a different path with Lindsay. Had he made the wrong choice all those years ago? Was the happiness he'd shared with Jennifer only an illusion, a fragile house of cards waiting to collapse?

"Jennifer, I…" he tried to say, but his voice was nothing more than a ghostly whisper, lost amidst the deafening noise of his conflicting desires.

"Killian!" she cried, her face crumpling with despair. She leaned forward, burying her head in her hands as sobs tormented her body. "I love you. I just want you back with me and the kids."

"Please, Jen," Killian begged silently, his voice a mere whisper amidst the flurry of emotions that threatened to consume him. "Hold on a little longer…I'll find my way back to you. I promise."

*****

Jennifer stood at the window, her gaze lost in the vibrant hues of the setting sun. The golden light bathed her face as if trying to offer warmth, but it did nothing to ease the chill that had settled in her bones ever since Dr. Cohen's visit. She clenched her fists, nails digging into her palms, as she fought against the waves of despair that threatened to drag her under.

"Mom?" a voice called from behind her. Jennifer turned to see her daughter, Hannah, standing in the doorway, and looking up at her with wide, innocent eyes.

"Hey, sweetie," Jennifer said softly, forcing a smile onto her face. "What's up?"

"Is Dad going to wake up soon?" Hannah asked, her lower lip trembling. "I miss him, and I am not ready to lose him."

Jennifer's heart broke at the sight of her daughter's tears, and she knelt down, pulling Hannah into a tight embrace. "I miss him too, honey. I wish I knew when he'll wake up, but—"

"Can't the doctors help him?" Hannah sniffled, burying her face in Jennifer's shoulder.

"Sometimes, even the best doctors can't find a way," Jennifer whispered, her own tears welling up as she held her daughter close. "But we have to be strong for Dad, okay?"

"Okay, Mom," Hannah mumbled, her voice muffled by Jennifer's sweater.

As Jennifer comforted her daughter, Killian's visions grew more intense and vivid, assaulting his senses like a storm raging within his mind. He saw Lindsay's face, felt her touch, and heard her laughter; memories that should have been locked away were now threatening to consume him whole. And as these visions grew stronger, so did his fear that they might somehow seep into his current life, tainting the love he shared with Jennifer and his children.

Please, don't let them take me away from you, Killian thought desperately, as if his silent plea might somehow reach Jennifer. *I need to be with you, with our family.*

In those quiet moments, when the weight of her decision pressed down upon her like a crushing burden, Jennifer found herself sitting by Killian's bedside, tracing the lines of his face with trembling fingers. She couldn't shake the memory of his eyes—once so full of life and love, now closed off to the world.

"Killian, I don't know what to do," Jennifer whispered, her voice cracking under the strain of her emotions. "How can I choose between letting you go and holding onto hope?"

Jen...I'm here. I'm fighting, Killian's thoughts echoed through the void that separated them, though he knew she couldn't hear him. *Just give me more time.*

*****

As Jennifer's desperation grew and the meeting with Dr. Cohen loomed closer, Killian's visions became a relentless torrent, merciless in their frequency and intensity. But amidst the chaos, he clung to the promise he'd made to himself: to find a way back to his wife, his children, and the life they'd built together.

Killian's heart raced like a trapped bird within his chest as another vision took hold, pulling him back into the past he thought he'd left behind. In this new memory, he stood on a cliff overlooking the ocean, with Lindsay beside him, her laughter a melody that echoed through the crashing waves below.

"Isn't it beautiful?" Lindsay asked, her eyes sparkling with excitement as she gazed out at the vast expanse of water.

"It is," Killian agreed, though his thoughts were consumed by more than just the breathtaking view. How could he reconcile the life he'd built with Jennifer and their children with these powerful memories of happiness and love shared with Lindsay?

He tried to focus on the present, to remind himself of the warmth of Jennifer's embrace and the joy in his children's laughter. But each vision that washed over him, each moment spent with Lindsay, only served to deepen the chasm between his past and present.

"Killian?" Lindsay's voice pulled him from his turbulent thoughts. "Are you okay? You seem… distracted."

"Sorry, I'm just—" He hesitated, struggling to put words to the confusion that swirled inside him. "I'm trying to make sense of everything that's happening."

"Maybe you're just not meant to understand," Lindsay suggested gently. "Sometimes, life throws us curveballs, and all we can do is trust that we'll find our way through."

As Killian stood there, the salt air clinging to his skin and the wind playing with Lindsay's hair, he couldn't help but wonder if she was right. Could he ever truly make sense of the visions that haunted him, or was his only choice to surrender to their relentless tide?

Meanwhile, the visions grew more vivid and detailed, unearthing long-forgotten emotions and memories. The feel of Lindsay's hand in his as they strolled along the beach and the taste of her lips as they shared a stolen kiss beneath the stars—all of it swirled around him, threatening to drown him in a sea of doubt and longing.

"Killian," Lindsay whispered one night, her voice a balm to his weary soul. "Do you ever wonder if we were meant for something more than this?"

"More than what?" Killian asked, though he could feel the weight of her words pressing against his chest.

"More than the lives we've chosen," she replied, her eyes searching his for answers he couldn't provide.

In that moment, Killian felt the ground shift beneath him as a question took root in his heart: Had he made a mistake in building a life with Jennifer? Had he left behind something truly special with Lindsay?

The thought gnawed at him, tainting the love he shared with Jennifer and his children. And as time slipped away, he knew he needed to find the strength to face his past and present—before it was too late.

Chapter 6

They Blinded Me with Science

The rain came down in soft sheets, its gentle patter against the windshield providing a soothing backdrop to Jennifer's troubled thoughts. The gray skies seemed an apt reflection of her internal storm as she navigated the slick, winding roads that led to St. Mary's Hospital. Her hands gripped the steering wheel with white-knuckled intensity, betraying her otherwise composed exterior.

As she pulled into the hospital parking lot, Jennifer caught sight of her own weary reflection in the rearview mirror. Her brown hair, usually meticulously styled, hung limply around her face, framing sharp eyes that were shadowed by dark circles. She sighed heavily and steeled herself for the meeting that lay ahead.

"Pull yourself together, Jennifer," she whispered to her reflection before stepping out of the car and into the damp embrace of the morning drizzle. Her heart pounded steadily against her chest, like the ticking of a clock as it counted down the moments until her appointment with Dr. Jeffrey Cohen.

Navigating the sterile hallways of St. Mary's felt strangely familiar to Jennifer, as she had walked them countless times before. Her heels clicked against the linoleum floor, each step feeling heavier than the last as she approached Dr. Cohen's office. Her breaths came in shallow gasps, as if she were drowning in the suffocating air that seemed to close in around her.

Jennifer hesitated outside the door, clenching and unclenching her fists in an attempt to muster the courage to face the man who held the answers to her husband's fate. The door handle felt cold and unforgiving beneath her trembling fingers, but she pushed it down and stepped inside, where the scent of antiseptic hung heavy in the air.

"Mrs. Flaherty," Dr. Cohen greeted her warmly, his voice a beacon of comfort amidst the storm raging within her. "Please have a seat."

"Thank you, Doctor," Jennifer replied softly, her voice betraying the tempest of emotions that threatened to consume her. Her eyes were drawn to the framed diplomas and certificates that adorned the walls, a testament to Dr. Cohen's expertise and dedication.

As she settled into the chair opposite Dr. Cohen's desk, Jennifer felt a gnawing sensation in the pit of her stomach, a mix of dread and hope, intertwined like vines that threatened to choke her. She stared at the doctor with wide, pleading eyes, silently begging him to provide some semblance of solace in this bleak moment.

"Doctor," she began, her voice cracking under the weight of her emotions. "Please tell me there is something we can do for Killian."

Dr. Cohen regarded her with a solemn expression, his kind eyes reflecting both sympathy and understanding. "I know how difficult this must be for you and your family, Mrs. Flaherty," he said gently. "And I promise you, we will do everything within our power to help your husband."

Jennifer's eyes darted around Dr. Cohen's office, taking in the meticulously organized bookshelves that lined the walls, filled with thick medical tomes and journals. The room was a blend of dark wood and soft lighting, providing an atmosphere of both professionalism and serenity. An elegant bonsai tree sat near the window, its branches reaching toward any sunlight it could find on the rainy day as if trying to escape the confines of the room.

"Mrs. Flaherty," Dr. Cohen began, folding his hands on the polished mahogany desk before him, "I understand that this is an incredibly difficult time for you, so I'll try to explain everything as clearly and simply as possible." He paused, allowing her a moment to brace herself for what was to come. "Killian's coma is caused by a severe brain injury," he continued, his voice steady and calm. "The damage has disrupted his brain's ability to communicate with his body. Essentially, his mind is active, he's alive, but his body is unable to respond."

Jennifer felt her heart clench at the doctor's words, each syllable driving another nail into the coffin of her hope. She blinked back tears, forcing herself to focus on the facts laid out before her. "So he's…trapped inside his own head?" she asked, her voice trembling.

"Unfortunately, yes," Dr. Cohen replied solemnly. "However, with the help of life support, Killian can continue to live indefinitely, although we cannot predict if he will ever regain consciousness."

A heavy silence settled between them as Jennifer absorbed the enormity of the situation. The sterile scent of antiseptic mingled with the faint fragrance of the bonsai tree, grounding her in the present moment as her thoughts threatened to spiral out of control.

"Is there any chance…any chance at all…that he could wake up?" she whispered, clinging to the last vestiges of her optimism.

Dr. Cohen hesitated, his eyes searching hers for a moment before he spoke. "There's always a possibility, Mrs. Flaherty. But I must be honest with you: it's highly unlikely. The extent of the damage to the motor skills area in Killian's brain is significant, and we've exhausted all available treatments."

Jennifer felt as if she were standing on the edge of a precipice, staring into an abyss of uncertainty and heartache. She blinked, willing away the tears that threatened to spill over, and took a deep breath to steady herself.

"Thank you, Dr. Cohen," she managed, her voice barely audible, even to herself. "Thank you for being honest with me."

As she stood to leave, the bonsai tree caught her eye once more—its delicate branches reaching for the light through the clouds, just as she reached for hope in this dark and uncertain time.

"Let me explain further," Dr. Cohen said, sensing Jennifer's need for clarification. He leaned forward in his chair, fingertips pressed together thoughtfully. "When a patient is in a coma with an active brain like Killian's, it means that they are technically alive and capable of multiple levels of thought. However, their earthly body is disconnected from their brain, rendering them unable to communicate or perform any physical actions."

Jennifer's brow furrowed as she processed this information, her fingers fidgeting with the edge of her blouse. The outside light filtering through the blinds cast streaking patterns on the floor, offering a stark contrast to the heavy burden that weighed on her heart.

"Dr. Cohen," she began hesitantly, her voice trembling slightly, "if Killian's brain is still active, then he must be…aware, on some level, right? What could he possibly be thinking while trapped in this state?"

The doctor's eyes softened with empathy, and he sighed deeply before responding. "It's difficult to say,

Mrs. Flaherty. Each patient's experience is unique, and we can't truly know what goes on within their minds. Some might be lost in dreams, while others may be reliving memories or experiencing something entirely different."

Jennifer's gaze drifted to the window, where wisps of clouds danced across the sky. She imagined Killian's mind, once so vibrant and full of life, now lost in a maze of thoughts and images she could never hope to navigate. A single tear slid down her cheek as she considered the possibility of him being trapped within himself, unable to reach out to her or their children.

"Is there…anything we can do to help him?" she whispered, desperate for even the smallest glimmer of hope. "Any way to bring him back to us, even if just for a moment?"

Dr. Cohen looked at her with a mixture of sorrow and compassion, clearly affected by her anguish. "I wish I had a more definitive answer for you, Jennifer," he said softly. "We will continue to monitor Killian's condition and provide the best care possible. In the meantime, I encourage you to talk to him and share your thoughts and feelings with him. Though we can't know for certain, it's possible that he may be able to sense your presence on some level."

"Thank you, Dr. Cohen," she whispered, her voice thick with emotion as she wiped at her eyes with the back of her hand. "I…I need some time to think about this."

"Of course," he replied gently, the empathy in his eyes a testament to the countless other families he had guided through similar heartache. "Take all the time you need, Jennifer. We'll be here to support you, whatever you decide."

The thought of being able to connect with her husband, even in the most tenuous way, brought a fragile sense of solace to Jennifer's heart. She stood, nodding her gratitude to Dr. Cohen, before quietly exiting his office, the weight of her decision still looming over her like an unrelenting storm cloud.

The weight of the decision seemed to crush Jennifer as she stepped out of Dr. Cohen's office, the door closing behind her with a soft click that sounded like a gunshot in her ears. The hospital hallway was a blur of sterile white and fluorescent light, the hum of distant conversations doing little to fill the silence that had settled over her like a shroud.

With each step, the cold linoleum floor felt more and more like slick ice beneath her feet, threatening to send her tumbling into an abyss of doubt and despair. She could feel the eyes of passing nurses and doctors on her, their concern a palpable presence in the air. But she couldn't bring herself to meet their gazes, afraid that if she did, the fragile dam holding back her tears would burst.

"Mrs. Flaherty?" A gentle voice broke through her thoughts, and Jennifer looked up to see Ann Fowler, one of the nurses caring for Killian standing before her, clipboard in hand. "Are you all right? You look…well, you look like you could use someone to talk to."

Jennifer hesitated for a moment, then nodded, swallowing hard. "Thank you, Ann." She managed to choke out, her voice trembling.

"Would you like to sit down?" Ann asked, gesturing toward a nearby row of chairs.

She sank into one, the plastic seat offering little comfort as she rubbed her palms together, trying to ease the chill that had settled deep within her bones. Ann took a seat beside her, her warm blue eyes filled with compassion.

"Sometimes, it helps just to say it out loud," she said softly. "To share the burden with someone else, even if just for a little while."

"I don't know what to do," Jennifer whispered, the words spilling from her like water from a cracked vase. "He's still alive, but…is it right to keep him here, like this?"

"Only you can make that decision, Mrs. Flaherty," Ann replied gently. "But I can tell you that whatever you choose, there's no right or wrong answer. You have to do what feels best for you and your family."

"Best for us—" Jennifer repeated, her gaze falling to her trembling hands as she fought back fresh tears. "How do I even begin to know what that is?"

"Trust yourself," Ann said softly, her voice a soothing balm against the storm raging within Jennifer's heart. "You know Killian better than anyone. You'll find the answer in time."

"Thank you," Jennifer whispered, the words barely audible as she stood slowly, steeling herself for the journey home. Ann gave her one last comforting smile before stepping away, leaving Jennifer to navigate the maze of halls alone.

As she stepped out into the crisp evening air, the world seemed to have shifted beneath her feet, its once-solid foundation now little more than shifting sand. She slid behind the wheel of her car, her fingers gripping it tightly as if it were a lifeline.

The drive home was a blur, the familiar streets transformed into unfamiliar territory by the weight of the decision that loomed over her like an ever-present shadow. As she pulled into the driveway and turned off the engine, Jennifer knew that the hardest part was yet to come.

For now, though, she had made it home, her sanctuary amidst the chaos that threatened to consume her. But even here, doubt lingered like an unwelcome guest, settling in the corners of her mind and whispering insidious questions that refused to be silenced.

Chapter 7

Is This a Dream

As days turned to months, Killian's conscientiousness pulled him further from Jennifer and closer to his life with Lindsay. He began to fill in the missing piece of his life with Lindsay.

The sun dipped low over the horizon, casting a warm golden glow on the charming Carolina coastal town. The scent of salt and sea filled the air, as seagulls squawked overhead. Nestled among white picket fences and fragrant rose bushes stood a beautiful two-story cottage that belonged to Killian Flaherty, his wife, Lindsay, and their two children, Jack and Emma.

As they walked hand-in-hand toward the house, Killian took a deep breath, savoring the simple beauty of this moment and the life he shared with his family. Despite the many challenges that came with his demanding career, he knew he wouldn't trade it for anything in the world.

For within the heart of this picturesque coastal town, Killian had found the true essence of love, happiness, and success, not only on the football field but also in the arms of his beloved wife, Lindsay, and their precious children.

"Another win today, huh?" Lindsay asked with a knowing smile. Killian had been coaching football for years, so she knew how much the sport meant to him.

"Yep," Killian replied, pride filling his voice. "The team played their hearts out."

Killian was a humble yet successful professional football coach known throughout the league for his expertise in cultivating teamwork. His portfolio boasted winning seasons and countless accolades, but what truly set him apart was his unwavering dedication to his players and the lessons they took with them off the field.

"Congratulations, honey. I know how hard you've worked with them," Lindsay said warmly, placing her hand on his knee. Her unwavering support and love were always present, and it reminded him of why they were a perfect match. She understood his passions and never failed to encourage him.

"Thanks, baby girl. It's not just me, though. The team has really come together this season, and I'm proud of each and every one of them."

"Of course, you are." She chuckled. "You're not just a great coach, Killian. You're also an amazing husband and father. Our family is truly blessed to have you." Killian smiled at her words, feeling both humbled and grateful. He glanced over at Jack and Emma playing and laughing on the front lawn. Their laughter and the warmth of Lindsay's hand on his knee were constant reminders that he had everything he could ever want.

"Hey, Dad!" shouted Jack from the front yard, his hands gripping a football tightly. "Can you show me how to throw a spiral like you do?"

"Sure, buddy," replied Killian with a warm smile, making his way toward his son. As he walked, he couldn't help but feel a sense of gratitude for the life he had built in this idyllic little town with Lindsay, who now sat on the porch swing, her laughter mingling with the sound of the waves.

"Okay, Jack," Killian began, positioning himself beside his son. "Hold the ball like this." He demonstrated the proper grip, guiding Jack's fingers into place. "Now, when you throw, make sure your elbow is up high and remember to follow through with your wrist."

"Like this?" asked Jack, mimicking his father's motion. Killian nodded approvingly, pride swelling in his chest.

"Exactly," he confirmed. "Give it a try."

Jack drew back his arm and released the ball with all his might. It soared through the air in a tight spiral before landing perfectly in Emma's outstretched arms. She beamed at her brother, clapping enthusiastically.

"Great job, Jack!" Praised Killian, ruffling his son's hair affectionately. They heard Lindsay's voice from her seat on the porch.

"Who's hungry for dinner?" she called out with a smile, her eyes glistening as they met Killian's.

"I am always hungry for your dinners, and I've got a hankering for your famous lasagna." Killian said, pulling himself from his thoughts.

Lindsay, her eyes sparkling with love. "But you have to promise to help with the dishes afterward."

"Of course!" Killian laughed, taking her hand as she stood up. "You've got yourself a deal, Mrs. Flaherty."

Together, they walked hand in hand into their cozy home, their hearts filled with contentment and love for the life they had created together.

As the family sat down to eat, Killian suggested, already looking forward to spending more quality time with his family, "After I get home from work tomorrow, why don't we take a walk along the beach after dinner? We can collect seashells and maybe even grab an ice cream at the ice cream shop on the boardwalk."

"Sounds perfect, Dad!" Emma chimed in, her eyes lighting up at the mention of her favorite ice cream parlor.

The Carolina coastal town was a haven of tranquility and beauty, nestled between the rolling waves of the ocean and the hills that stretched out behind it. Quaint shops and restaurants lined the cobblestone streets, their brightly colored storefronts a testament to the vibrant spirit of the community. The friendly residents greeted one another with warm smiles and genuine affection, making it the ideal place to raise a family and build lasting relationships.

As the sun set over the horizon, bathing the town in a golden glow, Killian took a moment to appreciate the picturesque scenery that surrounded them. The salty sea breeze brushed against his face, carrying with it the faint scent of grilling seafood from nearby restaurants. It was moments like these that reminded Killian just how perfect his life truly was, surrounded by his loving family, in a town that seemed to be crafted from dreams. In the end, it wasn't the number of victories on the football field that mattered most to him; it was the simple happiness he shared with Lindsay and their children that made his heart soar.

On Monday, Killian woke up to the gentle sound of waves against the shore. As he stretched and inhaled deeply, the salty taste of the ocean air mixed with the comforting scent of brewing coffee coming from downstairs.

"Morning, honey," Lindsay said, entering their bedroom with two steaming mugs. Her voice was like the warm sun kissing his skin, full of brightness and affection.

"Good morning, baby girl," Killian replied, taking one of the mugs from her hands with a grateful nod. The aroma of freshly ground beans and rich cream filled his senses as he took a slow, deliberate sip, savoring the robust flavor and the way it invigorated him for the day ahead. "This is perfect."

Lindsay teased, a playful glint in her eyes. "What would you do without your lucky cup of coffee?"

"Probably sleep in and miss all the action," he bantered back, wrapping an arm around her waist and pulling her close.

With a kiss just below her waistline, Killian rose from the bed and began to prepare for the day. He relished the familiar routine: the crisp feel of his coaching uniform, the supportive greeting from his fellow staff members, and the excited huddle of his team, eager for guidance and success. As he walked to his car, the town's natural beauty surrounded him, providing a serene backdrop to his daily commute.

Later in the day, as the sun began to dip below the horizon, casting vibrant hues of pink and orange across the sky, Killian made his way home. As the family gathered around the dinner table, sharing stories, Killian took a moment to reflect on his life. He had built a career doing what he loved, coaching others to be their best selves and cultivating a sense of teamwork. He had a loving wife and two amazing children who brought endless happiness into his world. And in the quaint Carolina coastal town, they were surrounded by beauty and warmth that seemed almost too good to be true.

The soft light of the setting sun filtered through the lace curtains, casting a warm glow on Killian and Lindsay as they sat side by side on their porch swing. The gentle creaking of its hinges harmonized with the distant sound of waves crashing against the shore, creating a serene backdrop for their quiet conversation. Killian's hand brushed against Lindsay's, their fingers intertwining as if to reinforce the bond that connected them.

"Remember our first date night in Charlotte?" Killian asked, flashing a nostalgic grin. "We got lost in each other's eyes, and for me, I knew right there that I found my soulmate."

"Ah, yes." Lindsay laughed. "It wasn't fancy, sharing a plate of nachos and then sitting in your car in the parking lot, but it was so magical sitting there with you, watching the stars come out together."

"Seems like a lifetime ago," Killian mused, his eyes filled with love and admiration for the woman beside him. Their weekend getaways had become cherished memories, from strolls along the boardwalk to afternoons spent swimming in the crystal-clear waters. Each adventure brought them closer, solidifying their passionate and loving relationship.

Their connection extended beyond those shared experiences, manifesting itself in the support they provided for each other. Whether it was Lindsay's unwavering encouragement of Killian's coaching career or Killian's dedication to Lindsay's painting, they were each other's pillars, fueled by an all-consuming love that burned brilliantly within them.

"Speaking of memories," Lindsay said, her voice a sultry whisper, "I can still feel the intensity of our lovemaking last night." She leaned in closer to Killian, her breath skipping a beat as she recalled their uninhibited passion. "It was...intoxicating."

Killian felt his cheeks flush at the memory, the vivid images of entwined limbs and the sensation of Lindsay's body pressed against his own sending shivers down his spine. "It's a testament to our love that, after all these years, we still share such a strong connection—physically and emotionally."

As night fell, the golden light giving way to twilight, Killian paused to take it all in—the sound of his children's laughter, the feel of Lindsay's hand squeezing his own, and the knowledge that they had built something truly special together. It was in those moments that he realized just how fortunate he was to have a life filled with love, happiness, and contentment, surrounded by those who mattered most.

The next day, as Killian stood on the sidelines of the football field, watching his team execute a near-perfect play, he couldn't help the pride that swelled within him. He saw the dedication and hard work these young athletes put into their training, all in the hopes of becoming better versions of themselves. It was moments like these that reminded him of why he loved coaching.

"Great job, team!" he called out, clapping his hands together with enthusiasm. "That's the kind of teamwork we need to win championships!"

"Thanks, Coach Flaherty!" One of the players shouted back, grinning widely as he jogged toward the bench.

Killian felt a warmth in his chest as he thought about the impact he had not only on the field but also in the lives of these young men. Praise from his peers in the league and the heartfelt thanks from former players who had moved on to successful careers—it all drove him to push himself and his team to be the best they could be.

"Coach, can I talk to you for a moment?" asked Tim, the team's wide receiver, as he approached Killian.

"Of course, Tim. What's on your mind?" Killian replied, turning his full attention to the young man.

"Ever since you took over as our coach, I've noticed such a difference in how our team plays and interacts," Tim said earnestly. "Your leadership has really inspired all of us to give our best every day. I just wanted to say thank you."

Killian felt a rush of gratitude and humility at the young man's words. "Thank you, Tim, but remember, I am merely a reflection of those I am blessed to work with. That said, hearing that means more to me than any trophy ever could. Keep up the good work, and let's bring home a championship for this town."

With a nod and a smile, Tim rejoined his teammates, leaving Killian to reflect on the immense satisfaction he derived from his work. As he watched his team practice, a feeling of contentment washed over him. He knew that beyond the field, his life was just as fulfilling.

As Killian walked through the front door of his home later that evening, the sound of laughter and the delicious aroma of Lindsay's cooking filled his senses. The joy and love within these walls were strong, and he knew that he had found the perfect balance between his passion for coaching and his devotion to his family. Killian stepped into the kitchen, where Lindsay was putting the finishing touches on dinner.

"Welcome home, honey," she greeted him with a tender kiss. "You look so happy."

"I am," he confirmed, wrapping his arms around her. "Everything I could ever want is right here in this moment. Hey, baby girl," Killian whispered in Lindsay's ear, "you up for a date night tonight?"

Lindsay held Killian tighter and whispered back "As soon as we put the kids to bed, I say we pour a glass of wine and see where the rest of the night takes us."

As her love enveloped him, Killian felt the veil between worlds begin to thin. The visions of Jennifer faded into the shadows, retreating to the realms of memory. His heart swelled with gratitude and hope, knowing that their love would guide them through the darkness and back into the light.

Killian stood at the entrance of his children's bedrooms, watching them with a tender smile as they slept. The soft glow of the nightlight cast whimsical shadows on the walls, painting a world of dreams and fairy tales. Their young faces were relaxed, expressions serene as if their souls had temporarily escaped to a place where worries did not exist.

"Good night, angels," Killian whispered, tucking the blankets snugly around their small forms. He placed a gentle kiss on each forehead, inhaling the comforting scent of baby shampoo that still lingered in their hair. Closing the doors behind him, he allowed himself a moment of quiet reflection. The love he felt for his children was overwhelming, a fierce protector dwelling within him, ready to defend against anything that threatened their happiness.

He made his way back to the kitchen, where Lindsay stood by the sink, her slender fingers diligently working away at the remnants of dinner. A cascade of blonde hair framed her face, capturing the warm glow of the overhead lights like a halo. She hummed softly as she worked, swaying her hips to an imaginary beat.

"Let me help you with that," Killian offered, stepping closer and reaching for a dish towel.

Lindsay looked up, her chestnut brown eyes dancing with laughter. "You've done enough, Killian. You deserve a break."

"No, but I insist," he said, his voice filled with playful determination. "After all, we're a team, aren't we?"

Her laughter tinkled through the air, mingling with the sound of water splashing against ceramic plates. "I suppose we are," she agreed, handing him a plate to dry.

As they worked together, the bond between them seemed to grow stronger, solidifying into something tangible that neither could deny. Killian marveled at how effortlessly they fell into sync, their movements mirroring one another like a well-rehearsed dance.

"Would you like some wine now?" Killian asked, already reaching for the bottle of Chianti they had been saving for a special occasion.

Lindsay hesitated, her eyes meeting his with a mixture of excitement and uncertainty. "I thought you'd never ask."

"Tonight feels like it deserves something a little extra, don't you think?" he said, flashing her a reassuring smile. "Besides, we've earned it."

"All right," Lindsay agreed, her voice barely audible above the sound of her own heartbeat.

Killian retrieved two glasses from the cupboard, cradling them in one hand while deftly uncorking the bottle with the other. Pouring the dark liquid into their glasses, he marveled at the way it seemed to capture the light, glistening like rubies as it swirled around the crystal. He handed Lindsay her glass, their fingers brushing against each other, sending a spark of electricity through both their bodies.

"Here's to us," Killian whispered, raising his glass in a toast.

"To us," she echoed, her voice soft and full of promise.

As they sipped the velvety wine, its warmth spread through their veins, igniting a fire that threatened to consume them both. The world outside faded away until all that remained was the beating of their hearts, the heat of their skin pressed together, and the knowledge that they were teetering on the edge of something powerful and magical.

The moon cast a silvery path over the dark, undulating ocean as Killian and Lindsay stepped onto the porch, their glasses of wine held carefully in their hands. The sea breeze caressed their faces, whispering secrets only the night could tell.

They sat in silence, the worn wooden bench creaking softly beneath them. Killian's hand found its way to Lindsay's leg, his thumb tracing gentle circles on her soft skin, drawing her warmth into him. The waves whispered in the distance, their rhythm providing a soothing backdrop to the thoughts swirling within them.

"Killian," Lindsay began, her voice barely above the wind's murmur, "have you ever wondered what brought us here? To this timeline?"

He gazed at her, his eyes reflecting the moonlight that dotted her silky blonde hair. "I've thought about it often, Lindsay. It's as if the universe conspired to bring us back together."

"Maybe it did," she whispered, her gaze locked with his, searching for answers in the depths of his soul. "Our connection seems to go beyond time and space, beyond anything we can comprehend."

Killian's heart trembled at her words, the weight of their significance sending shivers down his spine. He reached over and tucked a loose strand of her hair behind her ear, his fingers lingering on the delicate curve of her jaw. "There's something extraordinary about us, isn't there? I feel like I'm discovering a part of myself that's been hidden away all these years."

Lindsay placed her free hand atop his, her eyes glimmering with unshed tears. "Every time I look into your eyes, I see a world of possibilities, of love and passion that defy explanation. It's as though we're two stars drawn together by an unseen force, destined to collide and create something new and beautiful each time we are together."

"Like soulmates," Killian breathed, the word tasting like a revelation on his lips.

"Yes, like soulmates," she echoed, her voice filled with wonder and certainty.

They sat there, sipping their wine and sharing confidences neither had dared speak before. The ocean roared its approval, celebrating the unbreakable bond that was woven between them. In the silvered light of the moon, they recognized the truth in each other's hearts—that the love they shared transcended time, logic, and reason, binding them together in an eternal embrace.

Time seemed to dissolve around them as they sat on the porch, caught in the rapture of each other's gaze. The ocean breeze whispered its secrets, and the world beyond the veil of moonlight and shadow was forgotten. When Killian's hand tightened around his wine glass, Lindsay caught his eye and nodded.

"Let's go inside," she suggested softly, her voice a delicate tremor in the night air.

Killian hesitated for the briefest moment before setting down his glass and offering her his hand. As they stood and walked toward the house, their fingers entwined like coils of ivy, their hearts beat in silent harmony, a symphony of longing and desire that thundered through their veins.

The door closed behind them with the weight of a thousand unspoken words, casting them into the dimly lit sanctuary of their home. Moonlight filtered through the curtains, painting slivers of silver upon the walls and floor. They paused at the bottom of the stairs, their breaths mingling in the stillness.

"Are you sure?" Killian asked, his voice a low murmur laden with vulnerability.

"More than anything," Lindsay affirmed, her eyes shining with love and determination.

Their ascent to the bedroom was slow and deliberate, an intimate dance of anticipation guided by the soft creaking of the wooden steps beneath their feet. Upon crossing the threshold, Killian pulled Lindsay close, their bodies melding together as he pressed tender kisses along her collarbone and shoulders.

"Let me show you how much I adore you," he whispered against her skin, the heat of his breath sending shivers down her spine.

Lindsay responded with a sigh, her head leaning back in ecstasy as Killian's skilled hands began to undress her, tracing the curves and contours of her body with reverence. Each touch felt like a benediction, every caress a promise of the passion that would soon consume them.

As her clothing fell away, Killian guided Lindsay to the bed, laying her down upon the soft sheets before joining her. Their eyes locked once more, the intensity of their emotions reflected in the depths of their gazes. The world beyond the room ceased to exist as they gave themselves over to the fire that burned within them both.

"Let me pleasure you," Killian whispered, his hands tenderly exploring Lindsay's body, igniting a symphony of gasps and sighs from her lips. His touch was gentle yet insistent, drawing forth sensations she had longed to relive.

The slow build of desire reached a crescendo as they came together, their bodies entwined like two strands of a single soul. The world shattered around them in an explosion of color and light as they found release in each other's arms, their simultaneous climaxes a testament to the depth of their connection.

As their breaths slowed and their bodies stilled, Killian cradled Lindsay against his chest, his heart pumping with love and satisfaction. In that moment, as they had been before in other timelines, they were one, a union forged in passion and sealed by the knowledge that nothing could ever tear them apart.

The echoes of their impassioned cries still hung in the air, like the fading notes of a symphony that had reached its triumphant conclusion. The room was bathed in the soft glow of the moonlight filtering through the curtains, casting silver shadows on their entwined forms.

"Killian," Lindsay breathed, her voice barely audible above the sound of their mingled heartbeats. "That was…incredible."

He smiled down at her, his graying hair disheveled and his eyes alight with wonder. "It felt as if our souls were dancing together, didn't it?"

Lindsay nodded; her blonde hair fanned out against the pillow like a golden halo. "Yes, exactly. I've never felt anything so intense before."

As they lay there, wrapped in each other's arms, Killian's thoughts turned inward, reflecting on the profound connection he shared with this extraordinary woman. They had journeyed through many lives together, their paths weaving in and out like the threads of an intricate tapestry.

"I've always known you were my soulmate," Killian whispered, tracing the curve of Lindsay's cheek with his fingertips. "But tonight...It's as if all the doubts and uncertainties have been swept away, leaving behind only the purest essence of our love."

"Sometimes, words fail to capture the true depth of what we feel," Lindsay replied, her eyes shining with unshed tears. "What we experienced tonight transcends language. It is something that can only be understood by those who have lived it."

Killian's mind replayed the moments when they had reached their climaxes simultaneously, the sensation of their bodies merging into one, their spirits soaring to heights he had never thought possible. He knew now, beyond any shadow of a doubt, that their destinies were irrevocably intertwined.

"Every beat of my heart, every breath I take, belongs to you," Killian whispered, pressing a tender kiss to Lindsay's lips. "From this moment until my last breath, I am yours, and you are mine."

Lindsay smiled up at him, her eyes brimming with love and adoration. "And so it shall be, for all eternity."

In the stillness of the night, with only the gentle susurration of the waves outside and the soft rustle of the sheets as they shifted closer together, Killian knew that he had found his true home. For in the arms of Lindsay, his soulmate, he was complete, his heart finally at peace, his spirit free to soar into uncharted realms of blissful union.

Chapter 8

Danger Is Just around the Corner

Even in the waning light of the evening, Chris's laughter could be heard echoing across the backyard. Killian couldn't help but smile as he watched his friend. Chris was a hardworking man, with hands calloused from years of hard work and lines etched into his forehead from countless hours spent under the sun. But despite the long days and tiring work, there was an infectious joy that seemed to radiate off him. Perhaps it was the way his eyes sparkled with mischief after one too many whiskies or the way his booming voice carried across any room he entered; either way, it was impossible not to feel drawn to him.

"Killian! Come on over here, and get yourself a drink!" Chris called out, holding up a glass of amber liquid that shimmered in the fading sunlight. There was an inviting warmth in his tone, and Killian found himself making his way over to join his friend without even realizing it.

As he approached, Killian took in the scene before him: Chris's family gathered around a table laden with platters of sizzling steaks, plump sausages, and skewers of grilled vegetables. It was a testament to Chris's love of hosting family barbecues, a tradition passed down from generation to generation. For Chris, these gatherings were more than just a meal; they were a celebration of life, an opportunity to bring people together and create memories that would last a lifetime.

"Here you go, old friend," Chris said, handing Killian a glass filled to the brim with whiskey. The aroma wafted up to Killian's nose, a familiar scent that brought back memories of nights spent huddled around a roaring fire, swapping stories and sharing laughter with Chris by his side.

"Cheers," Killian replied, clinking his glass against Chris's, the sound ringing clear through the air like the chime of a bell. As they both took a sip, Killian felt the liquid warmth spread through his chest, bringing with it a sense of contentment that settled deep within him.

"Nothing like a good whiskey to take the edge off a long day, eh?" Chris said, his eyes crinkling at the corners as he grinned. There was something about the way he spoke that reminded Killian of the very essence of life—an undying love for adventure and an insatiable thirst for new experiences.

"Indeed," Killian agreed, his gaze lingering on the happy faces gathered around the table. It was in moments like these, surrounded by the people he cared for most, that he felt truly alive. And he knew that, in no small part, it was thanks to his dear friend Chris and his lust for life.

The sun dipped below the horizon, casting a warm glow over the scene as Killian and Chris stood side by side, their laughter mingling with the smoke that rose from the grill. In these moments, they seemed more like brothers than friends; their camaraderie forged not just through shared experiences but also in the striking similarities of their personalities. Both men were dedicated to their families and work, yet they possessed a playful spirit that brought balance to their lives.

Killian stood beside his friend, clapping him on the shoulder as they both took in the scene before them.

"Chris," Killian said, turning to the man beside him, "you've outdone yourself again."

Chris's eyes sparkled as he laughed, a rich and genuine sound that seemed to amplify the warmth of the fading sunlight. He was a hardworking man, dedicated to his job, but that didn't stop him from finding joy in the simple things in life. His love for a good time was rivaled only by his fondness for an occasional glass of whiskey, which he would often share with Killian during their late-night conversations.

"Ah, you know me, Killian," Chris replied, grinning from ear to ear. "I can't resist an opportunity to gather everyone together for some good food and better company."

Killian had known Chris for years, but every time he attended one of his friend's family barbeques, he couldn't help but marvel at how effortlessly Chris managed to bring people together. Despite his long hours at work, Chris never let it curb his enthusiasm for life. It was a quality that Killian admired deeply, finding solace in their shared appreciation of simple pleasures.

"Your family always looks forward to these gatherings," Killian observed, watching as children played around the lawn and adults chatted animatedly, their laughter mingling with the sound of clinking glasses and the sizzle of the grill. "It's a testament to your warmth and generosity, my friend."

Chris's cheeks flushed with a hint of pride, but he waved off the compliment. "Ah, it's nothing," he said modestly. "I just want everyone to have a good time, that's all. We need moments like these to remind us that there's more to life than just work and obligations."

Killian nodded in agreement, knowing all too well the weight of responsibility that bore down on him daily. He glanced over at Chris, who was now expertly flipping a steak on the grill, his movements fluid and confident. In that moment, Killian couldn't help but feel grateful for their friendship and for the little reprieve from his own worries that Chris provided.

"Here's to you, Chris," Killian whispered softly, raising his glass of whiskey in a silent toast. "And to many more barbeques beneath the setting sun."

Rapture of the Sleep

As the sun dipped below the horizon, casting a warm, golden glow over the backyard, Killian observed the way Chris's eyes lit up with joy as he interacted with his family and friends. It was in these moments that their connection was most palpable, the similarities between them shining like stars in the dusky sky. Both men were fiercely loyal to those they loved, placing their needs above all else.

"Come on, Killian!" Chris called out, laughing as he wrestled playfully with one of his nephews. "You're not getting away without playing a game of cards!"

"All right, you've convinced me." Killian chuckled, feeling the familiar surge of camaraderie that always accompanied their friendly competitions.

Killian followed Chris back into the house, the scent of grilled meat still clinging to their clothes. The kitchen table had been cleared to make room for a deck of worn cards, their edges softened by years of use. As they settled into their chairs, Killian couldn't help but notice how similar Chris's hands were to his own, strong and calloused from years of hard work yet gentle when necessary.

"High stakes tonight, my friend," Chris said with a grin, shuffling the cards expertly before dealing them out. "Loser has to clean up after dinner."

"Sounds fair enough," Killian agreed, his mind already calculating potential strategies as he surveyed the hand he'd been dealt.

As the game unfolded, their conversation ebbed and flowed like a slow-moving river, never quite touching on the deeper currents that ran beneath the surface. They spoke of mundane matters, politics, work, family, and shared memories, but each exchange was laced with an unspoken understanding, a mutual recognition of the struggles and triumphs that bound them together.

"Have I ever told you about the time I almost lost my job?" Killian asked, his voice shaded with a hint of nostalgia. As he recounted the story, Chris listened intently, his eyes never leaving Killian's face.

"Of course, I remember," Chris replied softly, placing a reassuring hand on his friend's shoulder. "You were terrified, but you faced it head-on, like you always do."

"Thanks to your encouragement," Killian admitted, feeling a surge of gratitude for the man sitting across from him.

As the game progressed and the night wore on, the quiet intimacy of their shared moments wove an invisible thread between them, strengthening the bond that had been forged over countless games of cards and shared experiences. And as Chris playfully declared victory, demanding that Killian make good on his promise to clean up, they both knew that beneath the laughter and friendly banter lay something far more precious, a connection that transcended time and circumstance, binding them together in a way few could understand.

As Killian stood at the sink washing the dishes, he clutched his head, the pain pulsating behind his eyes like a relentless drumbeat. The headaches had been growing in intensity and frequency over the last few weeks, plaguing him at all hours of the day. He could no longer ignore the nagging sensation that something was wrong.

"Damn it," Killian muttered under his breath, massaging his temples in a futile attempt to ease the agony. As he looked around, the unsettling feeling of being watched prickled at the back of his neck. It was as though someone was peering into the darkest corners of his soul, listening to his every thought and emotion.

"Hey, Killian, you okay?" Chris's voice cut through the fog of pain. Chris had been Killian's closest friend since he had moved to the coastal Carolina town, their bond forged through shared experiences and unwavering loyalty. They had seen each other through heartbreaks, successes, and everything in between, but the pain in Killian's eyes was a new experience for Chris.

"Chris"—Killian sighed with relief, grateful for the familiar voice—"I don't know, man. These headaches have been getting worse, and I can't shake this feeling that someone's watching me."

Chris wrinkled his brow, concern obvious on his face. "That doesn't sound good, buddy. Have you considered seeing a therapist? Maybe there's some underlying issue causing these symptoms."

Killian hesitated, rubbing the back of his neck. "I'm not sure, Chris. Therapy? Really?"

"Look, Killian," Chris replied earnestly, placing a reassuring hand on his friend's shoulder. "You've always been there for me when I needed help. Let me do the same for you. Give therapy a shot. What's the worst that could happen?"

Killian stared into Chris's eyes, searching for the courage to take his friend's advice. Finally, he nodded, resigned. "All right, Chris. I'll give it a try."

Chris smiled, relief washing over him. "Good. I promise it'll help, Killian. You deserve to be free of this pain."

The next day, Killian pushed open the door to Dr. Andrews's office. The room was bathed in soft, warm light coming from an antique floor lamp in the corner. The walls were lined with bookshelves filled with leather-bound volumes and framed diplomas. A time worn leather tufted leather armchair stood opposite a large mahogany desk.

"Hello, Mr. Flaherty, welcome," Dr. Andrews greeted him with a gentle smile. He was a tall man with salt-and-pepper hair and kind eyes that seemed to hold a well of wisdom. "Please have a seat."

"Thank you," Killian replied, sinking into the armchair as he nervously fidgeted with his hands. Dr. Andrews leaned back in his own chair, creating an atmosphere of calm and reassurance.

"Chris tells me you've been experiencing some troubling symptoms lately," Dr. Andrews began, folding his hands on the desk. "Why don't you tell me about them?"

Killian hesitated for a moment, then said, "I've been having these intense headaches, almost daily.

And I can't shake this feeling that…that someone's watching me."

"Interesting," Dr. Andrews pondered, nodding thoughtfully. "Now, there's something I need to explain to you, Killian. You've actually been in a coma for the past eight months, following a car accident. The impact resulted in a traumatic brain injury that has kept you deeply unconscious until now."

Killian stared at Dr. Andrews, his eyes widening in disbelief. "What? No, that can't be right. How am I here, talking to you?"

"Your mind is incredibly powerful, Killian," Dr. Andrews explained. "While your body remains in a comatose state, your consciousness has created this reality as a coping mechanism. What you're experiencing right now is taking place solely within your own mind."

"None of this is real?" Killian whispered, his voice trembling as he glanced around the room, desperately searching for something to ground him in reality. "But it feels so…vivid."

"Your brain has done its best to make this world as believable as possible, but sometimes, the truth slips through in the form of physical symptoms like your headaches and the sensation of being watched," Dr. Andrews said gently.

Killian shook his head, panic rising in his chest. "I don't understand. If I'm in a coma, how am I talking to you? How can I wake up? How can I get back to my real life?"

"First, you need to accept the truth about your situation," Dr. Andrews replied. "Once you've come to terms with that, we can explore ways to help you find your way back to consciousness within your earthly body. It's important that you trust me, Killian."

Killian took a deep breath, trying to calm the storm of emotions swirling inside him. "All right," he said, his voice barely audible. "I'll try. I just want to be free of this pain."

"Good." Dr. Andrews smiled reassuringly. "Together, we'll find a way to help you heal, Killian."

Killian's face went pale, and his hands trembled as he gripped the armrests of the chair. "So everything I've experienced with Lindsay…it's not real?" He choked out, barely able to form the words.

Dr. Andrews leaned forward in his chair, compassion etched on his face. "I understand that this is difficult for you to accept, Killian. But yes, your relationship with Lindsay is a product of your subconscious imagination."

"Then how did all this happen?" Killian asked, his voice quivering with anxiety.

"Your subconscious mind created Lindsay as a means to cope with the physical and emotional trauma of the accident," Dr. Andrews explained. "It happens occasionally in cases like yours where patients experience prolonged comas. The brain tries to fill the void by creating an alternate reality, one where you can find comfort and happiness."

"Even though it isn't real?" Killian questioned, tears beginning to well up in his eyes.

"Exactly," Dr. Andrews replied. "Your mind tried to give you what it believed you needed most, a loving partner and a life without pain. However, the fact remains that it's still just an illusion."

The weight of the revelation seemed to crush Killian's spirit. He slumped further into the chair, feeling the room spin around him. His chest tightened, and a heavy breath escaped his lips. "But it feels so real, Doctor. How can something that feels so true be nothing more than a figment of my imagination?"

"Your consciousness is incredibly powerful, Killian," Dr. Andrews said. "It has the ability to create vivid and lifelike experiences that can seem indistinguishable from reality. Your life with Lindsay has been carefully crafted by your subconscious to provide you with the love and support you crave."

"Is there any way to bring her into my real life?" Killian asked, desperation lacing his voice.

"Unfortunately, that's not possible," Dr. Andrews said gently. "Lindsay is a construct of your mind, and she cannot exist outside of it. The best thing you can do now is accept the truth and focus on healing from the inside out."

Killian wiped away the tears streaming down his cheeks, struggling to come to terms with the fact that the love he felt for Lindsay was nothing more than an elaborate illusion. He felt deep down that Dr. Andrews was right, but the thought of letting go of the woman who had brought him so much happiness felt unbearable.

"Where do we go from here?" Killian asked, his voice barely a whisper.

"First, we'll work on helping you understand and process your feelings about this revelation," Dr. Andrews explained. "Then we'll explore strategies to help you reconnect with your real life and the people who truly care about you."

As painful as it was, Killian knew he had no choice but to face the truth. It was time to let go of Lindsay and embrace whatever awaited him in the waking world.

As Killian wrestled with his emotions, a soft knock sounded at the door. "Come in," Dr. Andrews called out.

The door opened, revealing a woman with auburn hair that framed her face in gentle waves. Her hazel eyes, filled with concern, locked onto Killian's. Jennifer, his real-life wife, stood before him, her hands wringing together nervously.

"Jennifer," Killian whispered, his voice breaking under the weight of his pain.

"Killian," she replied softly, tears brimming in her eyes. "I...I didn't want to interrupt, but I just couldn't stay away any longer."

"Jen, I—" Killian started, but words failed him. His heart ached for the love he had for Lindsay, while his mind reeled with the realization that his actual wife, Jennifer, was standing before him.

"Is it true?" Jennifer asked tentatively, her voice trembling. "Everything you've said about...about Lindsay?"

"Unfortunately, it is," Dr. Andrews confirmed.

Jennifer hesitated for a moment before continuing. "I just don't know what to do anymore, Killian. You've been in this coma for so long, and your doctors are saying that...that your recovery is entirely up to you." Her voice cracked, and she swallowed hard. "They're suggesting that we...we consider removing you from life support if you continue to show no signs of waking up."

"Jen, I—" Killian began, but his voice faltered under the weight of the decision before them.

"Please, Killian," Jennifer pleaded, "tell me what you want."

"Jennifer," Dr. Andrews interjected gently, "it's important for both of you to process everything that has happened and for Killian to work through his emotions regarding Lindsay and his current situation."

Killian stared at Jennifer, his heart heavy with the knowledge that his imagined life with Lindsay was slipping away. At the same time, the reality of his life with Jennifer came crashing down on him.

"Dr. Andrews is right," Killian finally managed to say, his voice thick with emotion. "I need time to understand what's happening and figure out how to move forward. We...we can't rush the process."

"Of course," Jennifer agreed. "Take all the time you need, Killian. I'm here for you, but I also need to get on with my life, with or without you."

As Jennifer reached out to hold his hand, Killian felt both comforted by her presence and overwhelmed by the enormity of the situation. The road ahead would be long and difficult, but he knew that he could no longer hide from the truth. It was time to face reality and whatever it had in store for him.

The image of Lindsay's loving smile wavered in Killian's mind, slowly being replaced by Jennifer's tearful eyes. A heavy sigh escaped his lips as he struggled to make sense of the two lives that had become entwined within him.

"Killian," Dr. Andrews said softly, "it's natural for you to feel overwhelmed right now. The key to untangling these conflicting emotions is to acknowledge and validate them, rather than trying to suppress one or the other."

"Let's focus on your feelings first," Dr. Andrews suggested. "It's important to recognize that your emotions toward Lindsay are very real, even if the circumstances surrounding them are not. It's okay to grieve for that loss."

"Loss—" Killian muttered, staring down at his hands. "That's what it feels like. Losing someone I loved so deeply, and now, I'm facing the reality of a life with Jennifer. It's just…it's a lot to take in."

"Take a moment to breathe, Killian," Dr. Andrews advised, watching him carefully. "Remember, you don't have to figure everything out right away. Give yourself permission to process this new information at your own pace."

Killian nodded, and as he did so, images of both Lindsay and Jennifer flickered through his mind, each carrying their own unique set of memories and emotions. He could feel the love he shared with both women, and yet they were worlds apart.

"Dr. Andrews, how can I reconcile these two separate lives? How do I move forward knowing that one of them was never real?"

"Killian, it's important to understand that your subconscious life with Lindsay served a purpose. It helped you cope during a difficult time, and that's nothing to be ashamed of," Dr. Andrews explained. "As for moving forward, it's crucial for you to focus on the present and rebuild a strong foundation with Jennifer."

"Jennifer..." Killian whispered, his gaze drifting over to her. She offered him a small, encouraging smile, and he felt a flicker of warmth in his chest.

"Think about the connection you once shared with her and try to find ways to strengthen and nurture that bond. Communication will be key during this time, as well as fostering mutual understanding and support."

"Thank you, Dr. Andrews," Killian said quietly, feeling a bit more grounded. "I know it won't be easy, but I also know my conscientiousness cannot live in two separate worlds, so I'm willing to face whatever challenges lie ahead."

"Killian"—Jennifer interjected, reaching for his hand—"we'll get through this together, one step at a time. We've faced so much already, and I believe in us."

"Me too," he replied, giving her hand a reassuring squeeze. As he looked into her eyes, Killian knew that, despite the pain of losing his subconscious life with Lindsay, he had to return to Jennifer to remain alive.

Killian closed his eyes, with images of Lindsay and Jennifer again flooding his mind. "With Lindsay…everything felt perfect. We laughed, cried, indulged in pure passion, and shared our dreams. But it wasn't real." A tear rolled down his cheek. "And with Jennifer, we've had our ups and downs, but she's always been there for me, even when I was lost in the coma."

"Focus on those emotions," Dr. Andrews encouraged. "How do they differ when you think about Lindsay and when you think about Jennifer?"

"Whenever I think about Lindsay, I feel at peace, but now it's also shaded with sadness because I know that it was just a dream," Killian admitted. "But with Jennifer, I feel this connection, this bond that has weathered so much happiness but also pain and hardship. When I'm with her, I feel happy, stable, and secure."

"Remember, Killian," Dr. Andrews said, "making a choice doesn't mean you have to forget about Lindsay or invalidate the emotions you experienced in your subconscious life. It's about embracing reality and focusing on what's truly important now."

"Dr. Andrews is right," Jennifer spoke up, her voice cracking with emotion. "We can work through this together."

He looked into Jennifer's eyes, seeing the pain and love that they held. After a deep breath, he said, "I choose my life with Jennifer. I can't keep living in an illusion, no matter how much it hurts to let go of Lindsay."

"Are you sure, Killian?" Dr. Andrews asked, his eyes searching for any doubt.

Killian nodded, determination welling up inside him. "Yes, I'm sure. I need to focus on the reality of my life and work on rebuilding my relationship with Jennifer."

Jennifer's face lit up with relief, and she reached for his hand, gripping it tightly. "Thank you, Killian. I promise we'll make this work, together."

Dr. Andrews leaned back in his chair, nodding approvingly. "I believe you've made a wise decision, Killian. Acceptance is the first step toward healing, and I'm confident that you and Jennifer will be able to forge a strong, fulfilling life together."

Killian now sat alone in the dimly lit room, his heart pounding in his chest as he tried to process the information that had been thrust upon him. The room seemed to close in on him, the walls suffocating, as memories of Lindsay flashed through his mind like a reel of film. She was radiant, her eyes filled with love and understanding; she was everything he had ever wanted.

"Killian," Lindsay's voice whispered like a gentle breeze, resonating within the confines of his thoughts. "You know I'm here for you, and we will always find a way to be together."

The scent of lavender and jasmine filled the air, a comforting reminder of the woman who had captured his heart. Killian squeezed his eyes shut, trying to focus on the gravity of his decision.

"Killian, my love." Lindsay's voice caressed his ears. "Our time together has been nothing short of magical. But sometimes, the hardest choice is the one we must make for ourselves and those we love."

His heart ached as he weighed the options before him. He thought of Jennifer, the woman who was with him for so long even as their lives diverged. How could he abandon her to an existence lacking the love they once shared? Yet at the same time, how could he ignore Lindsay and the life they had built together in the sanctuary of his dreams?

"Is it fair to ask you to sacrifice your happiness for mine?" Killian wondered aloud, feeling the weight of his decision bear down upon him like an anchor.

"Killian," Lindsay's voice grew somber, "it's not about fairness. It's about finding the path that feels right for you and accepting the consequences that come with it."

"Thank you, Lindsay," he whispered. "No matter what happens, I'll never forget you."

"Nor will I forget you, my love," she reassured him gently. "Remember, whatever you choose, our love will endure."

Rapture of the Sleep

As Killian braced himself for the moment of truth, he felt a newfound resolve rise within him. The path forward would not be an easy one, but he was determined to see it through. No matter the outcome, his heart would carry the memories of both Lindsay and Jennifer, the women who had shaped his existence and made him whole.

Thunder rumbled ominously in the distance as Killian sat in the armchair clutching his head in agony as he waited for Dr. Andrews to return. Each heartbeat resonated through his skull like a hammer striking an anvil. The memory of Lindsay's tear-streaked face haunted him, her words echoing through his mind.

"Remember, whatever you choose, our love will endure."

"Killian!" Dr. Andrews called out, concern etched on his face as he rushed into the room.

"Doctor," he said, his vision blurring as vertigo threatened to topple him over. "I need…your help with transitioning back to my world with Jennifer."

"Of course," Dr. Andrews replied gently, putting his arm on his shoulder.

"Thank you," Killian whispered, his heart racing with a mixture of gratitude and fear. "Please just… make it stop," Killian begged, feeling the crushing weight of his decision pressing down on him like an avalanche.

"All right, Killian," Dr. Andrews began, "it is time for me to share all the details of your accident and condition so that you can easily transition back to your life with Jennifer." He pulled up a chair and sat down, his eyes meeting his. "I know this is going to be difficult for you to hear, but I need you to stay as calm as possible."

"You have been in a coma for the past eight months due to a car accident that left you with severe brain damage," he revealed, watching his face for any sign of recognition.

"Eight…months? I spent twenty wonderful years with Lindsay, how could I have only been in a coma for eight months?"

"Killian," Dr. Andrews interjected, "I understand how overwhelming this must be for you, but it's vital that you try to remain present and focused on what I'm telling you."

"Your mind has been trying to make sense of the trauma by creating an alternate reality for you," he explained. "It's not entirely unheard of, but your case is certainly one of the most complex and vivid that I've ever encountered."

As Jennifer stood over Killian's motionless body, her heart pounding, her fingers gripping the edge of the bed. The steady beep of the heart monitor hammered away at her resolve, echoing the relentless ticking of the clock on the wall. Her eyes flicked to the life support machine, the tubes snaking from its cold metal surface like veins of a mechanical leviathan.

"Killian," she whispered, her voice wavering. "I need to know you're still there."

As if in response, Killian's eyelids fluttered, his mind floating through an ocean of dreams and memories, desperately trying to find a beacon of truth amidst the stormy waves. He could feel Jennifer's presence, her voice cutting through his world with Lindsay like a dagger through his heart.

"Doctor," Jennifer called out, her voice hoarse, "please, can I have a moment alone with my husband?"

"Of course," the doctor replied, giving her a sympathetic nod before leaving the room. As the door clicked shut behind him, Jennifer sank into the chair beside Killian, her hands trembling as she clasped his.

"Killian, I love you more than anything," she choked out, tears streaming down her cheeks. "But I can't bear to see you like this anymore."

Please, don't do this, Killian thought, panic rising within him like a tidal wave. *I can fight this. We can face my two worlds together.*

"Eight months, Killian. Eight months I've prayed for a miracle, but…I can't keep our children waiting any longer. We need to move forward." She took a deep, shuddering breath. "I need to make a decision."

Jen, I understand the difficult decisions you have had to endure throughout this, Killian's thoughts pleaded. *It's you and the kids—our life together. Please don't take that away from me.*

"Killian," she whispered, her voice barely audible. "I'm so sorry." In that moment, as her fingers tightened around his, a spark of connection surged between them—a bridge across the chasm that had held them apart.

"Jennifer!" Killian cried out in his mind, his spirit reaching for hers.

"Killian?" Jennifer gasped, her eyes widening in shock. "Did you…?"

Jen, I'm here, he thought, willing her to hear him. *Please, don't give up on me.*

"Killian…" Her gaze held his, searching deep within his eyes for a trace of the man she loved. And then, like the sun breaking through the clouds after a storm, something shifted. "I'll find another way," she vowed, her tears mingling with fierce determination. "I won't let you go."

Thank you, Killian thought, relief washing over him. *Together, we can overcome this.*

"Stay strong, Killian," Jennifer whispered, pressing a tender kiss to his forehead. "We'll fight this, side by side."

It was then, as he watched her heart shatter before him, that the truth hit him like a thunderbolt. Jennifer was his reality: the life they had built together, their children who needed them both, all anchored by their love for one another. Lindsay was a beautiful memory, a remnant of another life he had already lived—but she was not his present. She was not his future.

"Jennifer," he whispered once more, this time with a newfound determination. "Please don't give up on me."

As if sensing his resolve, she looked up, her tear-streaked face searching for something—anything—to hold onto. And in that moment, Killian knew that together, they would find a way to bridge the chasm that separated them.

"Killian," she breathed, her voice barely audible. "I won't let you go. We'll get through this. I promise."

Chapter 9

A Different View

Jennifer sat on the edge of the couch in Carolyn's home, her fingers trembling as they fumbled with the clasp of her necklace. Her mind was a whirlwind of emotions, her heart heavy like an anchor. It was in this moment of vulnerability when she heard the soft footsteps approaching her from behind.

"Here, let me help you," came the gentle yet assertive voice of Jennifer's best friend, Carolyn. She had known Carolyn for over a decade, and their bond was unbreakable, forged through years of shared laughter, secrets, and heartaches.

Carolyn's fingers were deft and steady, a stark contrast to Jennifer's own shaking hands. As she worked on the stubborn clasp, Jennifer took a deep breath, inhaling the familiar scent of rosemary that seemed to cling permanently to Carolyn's clothes.

Despite her strong political opinions, which often led to heated debates between them, Carolyn possessed a loving nature that could set anyone at ease. Her empathetic spirit and warm smile were a balm for the soul, and Jennifer found herself grateful for her presence more times than she could count.

"Thank you," Jennifer whispered, feeling the tension in her shoulders ease ever so slightly as the necklace finally came undone.

"Of course, dear," Carolyn replied softly, her eyes meeting Jennifer's in the mirror. They held a depth of understanding and love that transcended mere words. "You know I'm always here for you."

Jennifer nodded, unable to hold back the tears that welled up in her eyes. "I just don't know what to do, Carolyn," she admitted, the weight of Killian's coma bearing down on her like a crushing force.

"Jennifer, my dearest friend," Carolyn said, her voice full of compassion, "you're doing everything you can. And I'll be right by your side, every step of the way."

The room was bathed in a warm glow, the afternoon light filtering through the delicate lace curtains that adorned Carolyn's living room windows. It was a space filled with history and memories, every corner housing an antique treasure or a rare artifact collected over the years. The walls themselves seemed to whisper stories of days long past, as if they too were privy to the secrets each object held.

"Look at this," Carolyn said, her eyes twinkling with delight as she carefully lifted a brass compass from the coffee table. "It belonged to a sailor in the 1800s. Can you imagine the adventures it must have seen?" Her enthusiasm for these relics was contagious, and Jennifer couldn't help but smile despite the heaviness that still lingered in her heart.

"Your collection has grown since I last visited," Jennifer commented, her fingers tracing the intricate details of a porcelain figurine. "You always seem to find the most fascinating pieces."

"Antique treasures tell us stories about our past, Jennifer," Carolyn explained, her voice laced with a fondness only a true collector could understand. "They remind us of where we've been and perhaps even offer a glimpse into where we're going."

As they continued to explore the room, Carolyn's thoughts drifted back to the present, her concern for her friend evident in the furrow of her brow. "Jennifer, I know things are difficult right now with Killian in a coma. But perhaps there's something you haven't tried yet."

"Like what?" Jennifer asked, her gaze settling on an ancient map that hung proudly on the wall.

"Have you considered attending a local support group?" Carolyn suggested gently. "There's one that meets weekly in the basement of St. Mary's Hospital. It's a safe space for people who are going through similar situations, and it might be helpful for you to share your experiences and feelings with others who can truly understand."

Jennifer hesitated, the thought of baring her soul to strangers both terrifying and oddly comforting. She knew she couldn't shoulder this burden alone any longer, and perhaps it was time to seek solace in the company of others who were walking the same painful path.

"Maybe you're right," Jennifer finally conceded, her eyes meeting Carolyn's once more. "It's worth a try, at least."

"Good," Carolyn said, her voice firm but gentle. "I'll come with you to the first meeting, if that would make it easier."

"Thank you," Jennifer whispered, feeling the weight on her chest lighten just a fraction. And as she stood amid the relics of the past, she couldn't help but wonder if somewhere among them lay the key to unlocking her own troubled future.

*****

The cold autumn wind rustled through the trees as Jennifer and Carolyn approached St. Mary's Hospital. The sun was setting, casting long shadows and bathing the old brick building in a warm, golden glow. It was both inviting and foreboding, much like the support group meeting that awaited them inside.

"Remember," Carolyn whispered as they entered the hospital, her breath forming small clouds in the chilly air, "you don't have to share anything you're not comfortable with. Just listen, observe, and take it all in."

Jennifer nodded silently, her heart pounding in her chest as her mind raced with thoughts of what lay ahead. She had never felt so vulnerable, yet she knew this was a necessary step on the path toward healing.

Descending the stairs into the basement, they followed the muted sounds of voices until they reached a dimly lit room filled with folding chairs arranged in a circle. At the center, a small table held a box of tissues and several cups of steaming coffee. A diverse array of people occupied the seats, their expressions solemn and their eyes weary from the weight of their own burdens.

The harsh fluorescent lights cast an unnatural glow over the sterile linoleum floor as Jennifer stepped hesitantly into the community center room. Her heart pounded in her chest, a heavy reminder of the decision that hung above her like a guillotine. The door clicked shut behind her, sealing her fate within those four walls.

"Welcome!" A soft-spoken woman with a tight smile and a clipboard greeted them as they entered the room, gesturing for Jennifer and Carolyn to take two vacant chairs. "We're just about to start."

"Thank you," Jennifer whispered, her voice cracking under the weight of her emotions. Across the room, she saw the circle of chairs filled with people who shared her pain. They were united by their burdens, each carrying their own cross to bear.

"Please have a seat," the woman said, gesturing to an empty chair beside a man whose eyes were filled with tears. Jennifer nodded and walked toward the chair, feeling the eyes of the others following her every move.

As Jennifer settled into her seat, she studied the faces surrounding her. There were men and women of all ages, each one bearing the scars of their unique struggles. She felt a strange sense of camaraderie with these strangers, knowing that behind each pair of eyes lay a story of pain and loss not unlike her own.

"Let's begin by introducing ourselves and sharing a little about why we're here today," the woman suggested, her voice compassionate and understanding. One by one, the members of the group spoke, their voices trembling with emotion as they recounted stories of loved ones lost or lingering in the agonizing limbo of a coma.

As the circle made its way around to Jennifer, she hesitated, her fingers gripping the edge of her chair as she fought to steady her nerves. "Hello, everyone," she managed, her hands wringing together in her lap. "My name is Jennifer, and my husband, Killian, has been in a coma for several months now."

"Hi, Jennifer," they all echoed back, their voices laden with empathy and understanding.

"Are you here to share your story?" asked the woman who had greeted her, now sitting across from Jennifer.

"Um, yes," Jennifer replied, swallowing hard. "I'm here because…I need some guidance. I've been told it's time for me to consider…taking Killian off life support."

Jennifer," the woman said gently, offering an encouraging nod, "we're here to listen and support each other, so please don't hesitate to ask for help or advice if you need it."

A heavy silence settled over the room, as if the air itself was thick with emotion. The man next to her reached over and placed a hand on Jennifer's arm, offering a comforting touch without words.

"Jennifer," he said softly, his voice strained, "I understand how difficult this must be for you. My wife, she's been in a coma for two years now. I've had to face that same decision more times than I care to count."

"Every day is a battle," chimed in a woman with tear-streaked cheeks. "I never imagined it would be this hard when my son was first injured. But we're here for each other, and that's what makes it bearable."

"Thank you," Jennifer whispered, her voice barely audible. She looked around the circle of faces, each one marked by their own personal struggle. They all understood the crushing weight that settled on her shoulders, the impossible choice she was being asked to make. Would they be able to help her find the answers she so desperately sought?

"Let's go around the room and share our stories," suggested the woman with the clipboard. "Maybe hearing from others will give you some perspective, Jennifer."

One by one, the people in the circle spoke, their voices cracking under the weight of their pain. They shared tales of hope and despair, of lives torn apart and rebuilt anew. And as Jennifer listened, she began to feel the tiniest glimmer of hope stir within her.

Maybe there is a way, she thought, as the man next to her squeezed her arm gently. *Maybe I can find the strength to make this decision…for Killian.*

As the last person finished sharing their story, Jennifer's gaze fell upon a woman with silver hair and kind, piercing eyes. She wore a pendant that seemed to catch the light as she moved, casting a soft glow on her face. The woman leaned forward, her hands folded in her lap.

"Hello, Jennifer," she began. "My name is Nora. My husband passed away two years ago, after several months in a coma. It was the hardest decision of my life, but I have come to find solace in the belief of multiple timelines where our conscientiousness can be free from our earthly shackles."

Jennifer's eyebrows rose slightly, her curiosity piqued. "Multiple timelines? How does that help you deal with your husband's death?"

Nora smiled gently, her eyes shining with warmth. "I believe that our souls (or conscientiousness) are eternal and that they continue to learn and grow through each life. When one life ends, our conscientiousness moves on to the next, carrying the experiences and lessons it has gained. It is my belief that as toddlers, we have the ability to recall our past lives and recall the loss of a life lived and all those close connections we had made. I feel a baby's cry is often for those they have let go of in a previous life. As we grow older, the memories of our past life fade away, and we build off our present earthly experiences to further shape our conscientiousness."

"Interesting," Jennifer whispered, her skepticism clear in her voice. "But how does that apply to Killian? He's not dead yet."

"True," Nora agreed, nodding thoughtfully. "But consider this: if the conscientiousness learns from each experience, then perhaps Killian's conscientiousness is learning something vital or reconnecting with a past life during his coma. By holding on, we might be allowing him to undergo a profound spiritual journey."

Jennifer crossed her arms, unconvinced. "That's a nice idea, but it doesn't change the fact that Killian's body is lying motionless in a hospital bed. His mind isn't working. He can't learn or grow like that."

"Ah, but our conscientiousness is not bound by the physical limitations of the body," Nora countered softly. "It is capable of great understanding and growth, even when the body is at rest."

"Even if that were true, it doesn't make this decision any easier." Jennifer sighed, her eyes welling up with tears. "How am I supposed to know what Killian's conscientiousness wants? How can I make the choice between life and death for him?"

"Sometimes, the hardest decisions are the ones that only we can make," Nora replied, her voice filled with empathy. "But remember, dear, our conscientiousness is resilient. Whatever path you choose, know that Killian's conscientiousness will continue its journey."

Jennifer chewed on her lip, pondering Nora's words. The idea of multiple timelines was a foreign concept to her, but it offered a glimmer of hope amidst her despair. Perhaps there was more to Killian's situation than she could see; perhaps his conscientiousness was learning and growing in ways she couldn't comprehend.

"Thank you, Nora," she whispered, her heart heavy with conflicting emotions. "I'll try to keep that in mind."

Nora leaned forward, her hands clasped together as if she were sharing a precious secret. "Think of our conscientiousness like a river," she began, her voice calm and soothing. "It's constantly flowing and changing, even when the surface appears still."

Jennifer furrowed her brow, trying to envision Killian's soul as a river. She glanced around the support group meeting room, taking in the faces of other attendees who were struggling with similar decisions. The atmosphere was heavy with emotion, and yet Nora's words seemed to cut through the tension, offering a sense of peace.

"Even during a coma," Nora continued, "the conscientiousness can continue its journey. Imagine a caterpillar cocooned within its chrysalis. On the outside, it may seem motionless, but inside, it is undergoing a profound transformation."

Jennifer's eyes widened at the analogy, her mind racing as she tried to apply this concept to Killian. Was his conscientiousness experiencing something profound, even though his body lay lifeless in that sterile hospital bed? She felt a spark of hope ignite within her chest, a feeling she hadn't experienced in quite some time.

"But how can I be sure?" Jennifer asked, her voice wavering. "How do I know if Killian's conscientiousness is truly growing during this time?"

"Sometimes, we must trust in what we cannot see," Nora replied gently. "Just as we cannot witness the transformation of the caterpillar into a butterfly, so too might we not fully understand the journey of a conscientiousness in a coma. But that doesn't mean it isn't happening."

Jennifer took a deep breath, her eyes glistening with unshed tears. She looked down at her trembling hands, clenching them into fists as she tried to absorb the weight of Nora's words. Was it possible that Killian's conscientiousness was on a journey she couldn't comprehend? That his spirit was learning and growing, even as his body lay inert?

"Thank you," Jennifer whispered, her voice barely audible. "I never thought of it that way before."

"Sometimes, a different perspective can bring us the peace we need in difficult times," Nora said with a warm smile. "Remember, dear, the conscientiousness is resilient and will find its way no matter what obstacles it encounters."

Jennifer nodded, her heart swelling with newfound hope and determination. She would carry Nora's words with her, a beacon of light guiding her through the darkness of her decision. And though the path ahead remained uncertain, she could at least take solace in the belief that Killian's conscientiousness was on a journey all its own, one that continued to grow and learn, despite the stillness of his earthly form.

Jennifer gazed around the room, her eyes drawn to the other attendees who sat huddled in small groups or alone, like islands adrift in a sea of grief. The support group met in the basement of St. Mary's Church, a dimly lit space with low ceilings and exposed pipes that seemed to amplify the heavy air of sadness that hung over them all. A few flickering candles on a nearby table cast soft shadows upon the walls, providing the only source of light apart from the narrow, grated window that allowed in scant slivers of daylight. The scent of dampness mixed with the faint aroma of burnt wax permeated the air, becoming an olfactory testament to the sorrows each person carried within.

"May I ask you something?" Jennifer began hesitantly, her voice slightly trembling as she turned back to Nora. "Do you think...do you believe that if we remove someone's life support, their conscientiousness' journey might be cut short?"

Nora leaned back in her chair, pondering the question for a moment before responding. "I don't pretend to know all the answers, dear," she said softly. "But I believe that when it is time for a conscientiousness to move on, it will. Our physical bodies are just vessels, after all."

"Killian's been in a coma for months now. I've been trying to hold onto hope that he'll wake up, but the doctors...they say his chances are slim." Jennifer paused, taking a shaky breath. "I'm afraid that if I let him go, I'm failing him somehow."

"Life and death are beyond our control," Nora said gently, reaching out to place a comforting hand on Jennifer's knee. "What matters most is the love we give and the lessons we learn while we're here. You have shown Killian great love and devotion, Jennifer. Remember, our conscientiousness is eternal, even if our bodies are not."

Jennifer nodded, allowing herself to consider the possibility that Killian's conscientiousness had its own journey to travel, regardless of what she decided for his physical body. "Do you think we'll see our loved ones again in another life?"

"Perhaps," Nora replied with a smile, her eyes shining with a tender wisdom. "I like to believe that each conscientiousness who share a deep connection will always find their way back to each other, in one form or another."

The words seemed to resonate within Jennifer, striking a chord deep within her heart. As she looked around the room once more, she saw the faces of the others now etched not just with grief but also with hope, a testament to the power of shared burdens and the comfort of human connection.

"Thank you, Nora," Jennifer whispered, feeling an unexpected sense of peace begin to settle over her. "Your insights have given me something new to hold onto."

"Sometimes, all it takes is a little shift in perspective to help us find our way through the darkness," Nora said softly, giving Jennifer's hand a gentle squeeze before releasing it. "I'm glad I could help. Remember that no matter what happens, love transcends all boundaries."

"Excuse me, everyone," Jennifer announced softly, standing up from her chair with renewed determination. "I need to go. There's something I must do, for Killian and myself."

Whispers of encouragement and understanding rippled through the group. Jennifer felt a weight lift from her shoulders, buoyed by the support and empathy of these strangers who had become her lifeline through this difficult time.

"Good luck, Jennifer," Nora whispered, giving her a final reassuring squeeze.

"Thank you," Jennifer replied, her voice stronger than it had been in weeks. She walked toward the door, feeling the heaviness of her burden lighten with each step. As she reached for the handle, she paused, turning back to address the entire group. "And thank you all for sharing your stories and your strength."

With that, she and Carolyn stepped out into the cool night air, her heart swelling with newfound hope. As they walked to the car, Jennifer considered her next steps. "Do you want to go someplace to grab a tea and chat about what we just heard?" she asked Carolyn.

"That would be great. I would love to hear your thoughts on what we just experienced as well as what Dr. Cohen shared with you," Carolyn quickly responded.

*****

The bell above the door chimed softly as Jennifer and Carolyn stepped into the quaint café, their eyes adjusting to the warm and cozy interior. Aromas of freshly brewed tea and buttery pastries filled the air, instantly evoking a sense of familiarity and comfort for the two women. The café was adorned with mismatched antique china and lace tablecloths, giving it an old-world charm that seemed to slow down time amidst the chaos of the outside world.

"Isn't this place lovely?" Carolyn whispered as they made their way to a secluded corner table by the window, her breath fogging up the glass momentarily. "I always feel like I've stepped back in time when I come here."

Jennifer smiled weakly, her thoughts still consumed by Killian's condition and the weighty decision that lay ahead of her. She carefully sat down, her hands trembling slightly as she reached for the ornate teapot at the center of the table. As she poured the steaming liquid into delicate porcelain cups, she could feel the heat radiating through the china, warming her cold fingers. It was a small comfort that reminded her just how much she needed a moment of respite from her own swirling thoughts.

"Jennifer, you know you can talk to me about anything," Carolyn said gently, reaching out to place a reassuring hand on her friend's arm. "How are you holding up?"

Taking a deep breath, Jennifer set down the teapot and looked into Carolyn's empathetic eyes. "It's just…so difficult to wrap my head around everything," she admitted, her voice barely more than a whisper. "Dr. Cohen explained to me that Killian's brain is still very much alive and functioning, even though he's in a coma."

"Alive?" Carolyn echoed with surprise, leaning in closer to hear the details.

Jennifer nodded, her eyes brimming with unshed tears. "Yes, alive. Dr. Cohen said that in Killian's mind, he might be living and experiencing a whole other life, possibly even feeling happiness. But his earthly body is just...trapped, unable to move or communicate."

The gravity of the situation settled over their small corner like a heavy shroud, muffling the ambient sounds of the café. Carolyn squeezed Jennifer's hand, her eyes filled with compassion.

"Jennifer, I can't imagine how hard this must be for you," she whispered, her voice filled with genuine empathy. "But whatever decision you make, know that I am here for you every step of the way."

A single tear trickled down Jennifer's cheek as she stared at the intricate patterns of the lace tablecloth, her heart aching with both gratitude for Carolyn's unwavering support and the immense burden of her husband's uncertain future. The steaming cups of tea before them seemed to mirror the warmth of their friendship, offering solace against the cold reality of life's harshest challenges.

The scent of rose petals drifted through the air, a soft counterpoint to the quiet hum of conversation within the quaint cafe. Jennifer stared down into her cup of tea, watching the delicate leaves unfurl and swirl in the steaming water as if they were engaged in a graceful dance. The hushed words of comfort and understanding shared by the other members of the support group echoed in her mind, their stories blending together like the intricate flavors of her tea.

"Jennifer," Carolyn said softly, drawing her out of her daydream. "I can see you're lost in thought. What's on your mind?"

Jennifer hesitated for a moment before speaking, her voice barely audible above the bustling leaves outside. "At the support group today, they discussed the concept of multiple timelines. I've never really given it much thought before, but now…now it's all I can think about."

"Multiple timelines is tough to wrap my head around?" Carolyn stated, curiosity piqued as she leaned closer, her own cup of tea momentarily forgotten.

"Yes," Jennifer continued, her gaze shifting to the raindrops that clung to the windowpane beside them. "Like Nora said, the idea that our souls continue on after we leave this life, only to be reborn again in a new body. That maybe, just maybe, Killian's soul is already yearning to move on, to experience another life filled with love and laughter."

A heavy silence settled between them, broken only by the rhythmic tap of raindrops against the glass. Jennifer could feel the weight of her decision pressing down upon her, an unbearable burden that threatened to crush her spirit beneath its merciless force. The pain of choosing between holding onto the man she loved and allowing him the chance to live again, even if it meant leaving her behind, was a torment she had never imagined possible.

"Jennifer," Carolyn whispered, her hand reaching across the table to rest gently atop her friend's trembling fingers. "No one can make this decision for you, but I believe that whatever choice you make will be the right one, for both Killian and your family."

Closing her eyes against the swell of tears threatening to spill over, Jennifer drew in a shuddering breath, the aroma of roses and sorrow filling her senses. The pain was all-consuming, a storm raging within her heart that left her feeling as battered and broken as the autumn leaves that fluttered helplessly on the winds outside.

"Thank you, Carolyn," she whispered, her voice barely audible above the noise of her thoughts. "I just…I just don't know if I can let him go."

"Take your time, my dear," Carolyn reassured her, her touch a beacon of warmth amidst the shadows of uncertainty that surrounded them. "You have our love and support, no matter what you decide."

For a moment, Jennifer and Carolyn sat in silence. The tea had taken on a lukewarm temperature, and the scones were little more than crumbs scattered on their plates.

"Jennifer, I want to remind you that you're not alone in this," Carolyn said softly, her gaze never leaving Jennifer's face. "I'm here for you, every step of the way. No matter what decision you make, I'll always be by your side."

Jennifer looked up at Carolyn, her eyes glistening with unshed tears as she tried to summon a faint smile. "You have no idea how much that means to me," she whispered, feeling the weight of the decision bearing down on her shoulders ever so slightly ease.

"Of course, my dear." Carolyn reached out, giving Jennifer's hand a reassuring squeeze. "Now, why don't we head home? It's getting late, and I think both of us could use some rest."

Nodding her agreement, Jennifer carefully wiped away the last remnants of her tears before rising from the table. As they stepped outside, the vibrant hues of red and gold in the trees seemed almost to offer solace in the face of the heartache that loomed over her like a storm cloud.

The drive back to Carolyn's antique colonial home was a quiet one, the hum of the car's engine the only sound breaking the stillness. Though Jennifer's hands remained steady on the wheel, her thoughts churned like the fallen leaves caught in swirling wind around them. She couldn't help but wonder what Killian would want, would he choose to remain in his coma, knowing that it left him trapped between worlds, or would he embrace the possibility of rebirth, even if it meant leaving behind everyone he loved?

As Jennifer turned onto the gravel driveway that led to Carolyn's home, the sight of the stately house brought a fleeting sense of peace. The elegant structure, with its weathered clapboard and ivy-covered walls, seemed to embody the passage of time, a testament to the resilience of love and devotion.

"Thank you, Carolyn," Jennifer whispered as they pulled to a stop before the entrance. "For everything."

"Anytime," Carolyn replied, her voice thick with emotion. "You're like a sister to me, Jennifer."

With a final embrace, they parted ways, each retreating to their respective sanctuaries, one to wrestle with the weight of an impossible decision and the other to lend her unwavering support from afar. And yet despite the miles and uncertainties that separated them, the bond between Jennifer and Carolyn remained as steadfast and unbreakable as the ancient oak that stood outside Carolyn's antique colonial home, its roots entwined with the very essence of the earth itself.

As Jennifer started the engine to head home, her thoughts swirled with possibilities and plans. The road ahead was still uncertain, but now she had powerful knowledge and friendships to guide her, the belief that love could triumph over even the darkest of circumstances and that in their own ways, both she and Killian would continue to grow and learn. With renewed faith, she drove away from Carolyn's home, ready to face whatever challenges lay ahead.

Chapter 10

Self-Discovery

As Jennifer was becoming more aware of the multiple-timeline possibilities, Killian was also on a quest to discover how his conscientiousness was blending across multiple lives he has lived, and as the sun dipped low in the sky, Killian sat on a park bench, his fingers tapping nervously against the coarse wooden planks beneath him. The sounds of laughter and distant conversations from passersby seemed to fade into the background as he turned his thoughts inward.

"Killian, are you even listening?" Lindsay's voice broke through his daydream, her chestnut brown eyes wide with concern.

"Sorry, I just…I have a lot on my mind," he admitted, raking a hand through his salt-and-pepper hair.

"Talk to me." Lindsay reached out and gently placed her hand on his, stilling his fidgeting fingers.

Killian hesitated, unsure if he could find the words to accurately convey the turmoil within him. His life felt like a tangled web of contradictions, human experiences mingling with spiritual ones in a way that left him feeling unmoored.

"Ever since we discovered our connection to the spiritual world, I've been struggling to reconcile my two lives," he began cautiously. "I feel like I'm being pulled in opposite directions, and it's tearing me apart."

"Have you considered seeking guidance? My friend Silas has a lot of knowledge with multiple timelines and may be able to help you navigate this," Lindsay suggested softly, her thumb tracing soothing circles on the back of his hand.

He looked at her, grateful for her unwavering support but doubting whether anyone could truly understand the complexity of his situation. "I just don't know enough about the nature of human consciousness or its connection to the physical and spiritual worlds. How can I make an informed decision about my future without understanding how it all fits together?"

Lindsay sighed, worry etching lines into her otherwise youthful face. "That's a valid point, Killian. But maybe you don't need to figure it all out on your own. Silas and others have walked this path before you."

Killian mulled over her words, his gaze drifting to the vibrant flowers that bloomed around them. Perhaps she was right, maybe there were wise souls who could help him navigate this treacherous path and ultimately make a decision about his future.

"Maybe you're right," he conceded, feeling the first flicker of hope in what felt like an eternity. "How do I find Silas? Can you help introduce me to him?"

"Start with your dreams," Lindsay whispered, a knowing smile playing on her lips. "They're the gateway to our past lives and to the wisdom we've accumulated over countless lifetimes. From there, Silas will find you."

"Thank you, Lindsay," Killian whispered, giving her hand a grateful squeeze. As the sun slipped below the horizon, he felt a renewed sense of determination take root within him. No longer content to remain adrift in uncertainty, he resolved to seek out the answers he so desperately craved, whatever it might take.

That night, Killian lay in bed, the moonlight casting a silvery glow on his disheveled hair. He closed his eyes and tried to focus on his breathing, willing himself into a dream state where he might find the guidance he sought. As sleep began to take hold, he felt a subtle shift in his consciousness, like a door opening to another realm.

The world that materialized around him was magical and shaded with an otherworldly beauty. Lush gardens bloomed beneath a sky painted with hues of twilight, and a gentle breeze carried the scent of lilacs and jasmine. In the distance, a group of figures approached, their feet barely touching the ground as they floated toward him.

"Welcome back, Killian," said the first figure, her voice melodious and soothing. She had long, flowing hair the color of midnight, and her eyes sparkled with the wisdom of countless lifetimes. "I am Aria, a soul who once walked beside you and Lindsay."

"Thank you, Aria," Killian replied, feeling a sense of familiarity wash over him. He sensed that these souls were indeed the wise guides he'd hoped to encounter.

"Allow me to introduce my companions." Aria gestured toward the others. "This is Silas, who bears the knowledge of the universe's mysteries," she said, pointing to a tall, slender man with pure white hair and eyes that seemed to hold the secrets of the cosmos. "And this is Elara, who understands the intricate dance between our physical and spiritual selves." Elara appeared before him, her delicate features framed by cascades of copper curls, her emerald green eyes radiating empathy and compassion.

"Each of us has crossed paths with you in past lives, Killian," Silas explained, his voice filled with a quiet authority. "We have come to share our collective wisdom and help guide your journey."

"Thank you," Killian said, his heart swelling with gratitude. He knew that time was of the essence, so he wasted no words. "I am struggling to reconcile my human life and spiritual existence. I feel as if I am being torn in two directions, and I don't know which path to choose."

"Ah, a struggle many souls have faced," Elara whispered, her eyes filled with understanding. "It is important to remember that we exist in both realms simultaneously—our physical bodies are mere vessels for our consciousness, while our true selves reside in the spiritual world."

"Your journey is one of self-discovery and growth," Aria added. "The answers you seek lie within, but we can help illuminate the path ahead."

As they spoke, Killian felt a sense of clarity slowly begin to unfold within him. These wise souls offered insights into the nature of human consciousness and its connections to the physical and spiritual worlds. They revealed how he could harness his innate gifts to create harmony between these seemingly disparate aspects of his existence.

"Thank you," Killian whispered, tears of gratitude welling up in his eyes. "Your guidance has given me the strength and the courage to face my future, whatever it may hold."

"Remember, Killian," Silas said, his gaze penetrating the depths of Killian's soul. "You are never alone on this journey. We will always be here to guide you when you need us."

A soft, cool breeze rustled the leaves of the ancient oak tree under which Killian sat, its massive branches reaching out like protective arms. He took a deep breath, inhaling the earthy scent of the moss-covered ground beneath him. The steady rhythm of his heartbeat seemed to synchronize with the gentle swaying of the branches above.

"Killian," Silas whispered, his melodious voice echoing through the air, "there is still much for you to understand. One of the fundamental aspects of our existence is the cycle of reincarnation."

As the words left Silas's lips, a warm, vibrant energy enveloped Killian, and he found himself transported to a realm where time seemed to stand still. Awe filled his being as he observed swirling masses of color that collided and merged, creating intricate patterns of pulsating light. He could feel the presence of the otherwise souls around him, their energies combining to form a symphony of knowledge and understanding.

"Reincarnation," began Aria, her luminescent form shimmering in front of Killian, "is the process by which our consciousness merges with new human bodies after the end of one physical life. As we live countless lives, we gather experiences and wisdom, shaping our souls on a continuous journey toward enlightenment."

"Each new life," chimed in Elara, "is an opportunity to learn, to grow, and to balance the karmic scales. Our past deeds, both good and bad, influence our present circumstances and the challenges we face."

Images flashed before Killian's eyes: warriors locked in battle, a mother cradling her child, and a healer tending to the sick. He saw himself in each scene, different bodies and different lives but the same soul.

"Your current life, Killian," Silas said gently, "is deeply connected to those you've lived before. There are patterns and familiar faces that reappear, leading you to the experiences you need for your soul's growth."

"Like Lindsay," Killian thought aloud, as the memory of their past life together swirled through his mind. "Our love transcends lifetimes."

"Indeed," Aria confirmed with a soft smile. "Your bond with Lindsay is one that has been forged over many lives, each time growing stronger, helping both of you on your individual paths."

"Is there a way to remember these past lives more clearly?" Killian asked, yearning to understand all the experiences that had shaped him.

"Sometimes, memories may surface spontaneously or through deep meditation," Elara explained. "But it is not necessary to recall every detail. The lessons and wisdom gained are carried within you, even if you can't consciously remember them."

"Your journey through the cycle of reincarnation is an intricate tapestry, interwoven with countless threads," Silas said. "Each life adds another layer of complexity and beauty to your soul."

Killian felt a profound sense of wonder and humility at the vastness of his own existence. It was as if he could suddenly perceive the intricate web of connections between his past, present, and future lives, a kaleidoscope of experiences stretching out in every direction.

"Thank you," he whispered, feeling a renewed sense of purpose and resolve. "I will carry this knowledge with me, as I strive to create harmony between my human life and my spiritual nature."

"Remember, Killian," Aria said, her voice shaded with warmth, "the wisdom lies within you, waiting to be discovered."

The vibrant realm of light began to recede, and Killian found himself once again beneath the ancient oak tree. The sun now hung low in the sky, casting long shadows across the ground. As he gazed up at the branches above him, Killian felt the weight of centuries, the countless lives he had lived, and the endless possibilities that lay before him. He was ready to embrace his destiny, guided by the wisdom of the wise souls and the eternal journey of his soul through the cycle of reincarnation.

Killian sat on the edge of his bed, his fingers tracing the embroidered pattern on the quilt. The soft glow from the bedside lamp cast warm shadows across the room. Soft whispers from Silas and Aria resonated in his mind, their words dancing like fireflies in a summer night.

"Tell me more about exploring past lives in dreams," Killian asked, his voice hushed with anticipation. "How does that work?"

"Your dream state," Silas began, "acts as a bridge between your conscious and subconscious mind. Through it, you can access memories from your past lives."

"Think of it as a key to unlock the door to your soul's history," Aria added. "In your dreams, you can explore the events, emotions, and relationships that have shaped your spirit over countless lifetimes."

"Is there a method I should follow?" Killian inquired, eager to learn more.

"Before you go to sleep," Silas instructed, "focus on a specific question or aspect of your life you wish to gain insight into. Hold that intention in your mind as you drift off, and allow your consciousness to guide you through the maze of your past lives."

"Be cautious, though," Aria warned, her voice gentle but firm. "These explorations can bring both enlightenment and pain. You must be prepared to face whatever truths you uncover."

Shivers ran down Killian's spine, but he nodded, determined to forge ahead. That night, as he lay in bed, he focused on his relationship with Lindsay, wondering how it had been influenced by their shared past lives. He felt himself sink into the velvety darkness of sleep, his consciousness threading its way through time and space.

The landscape of his dream world opened before him. He found himself standing in a bustling marketplace, surrounded by vibrant colors, enticing aromas, and the sounds of voices from a thousand different conversations. As he walked, the scene shifted around him, morphing into a moonlit garden, where he and Lindsay danced beneath an indigo sky.

"Remember this, Killian?" Lindsay whispered, her chestnut brown eyes sparkling with mischief. "We were lovers in seventeenth-century France."

Killian gazed into her eyes, suddenly recalling their secret rendezvous, stolen kisses, and the passion that had bound them together despite societal constraints.

The dream continued to unfold, revealing more past lives shared with Lindsay. They were siblings in ancient Rome, warriors fighting side by side in a fierce battle. In another life, they were bitter rivals, their animosity spanning decades until death separated them.

Each memory was like a piece of a puzzle, painting a broader picture of their eternal connection. Killian began to understand how their previous experiences had influenced their current relationship, shaping it in subtle yet profound ways.

As dawn approached, Killian's consciousness began to retreat from the dream world. He opened his eyes to find himself back in his bedroom, the first light of morning streaming through the curtains. He lay there, awash in the memories of his past lives, feeling both humbled and invigorated by the vastness of his existence.

"Thank you," he whispered to Silas and Aria, who seemed to be listening from the corners of his mind. "Dreams have shown me the rich tapestry of my soul's journey."

"Embrace these memories, Killian," Silas encouraged. "They are the keys to unlocking your full potential and understanding the true nature of your spirit."

"Remember," Aria added, "the choices you make today will shape your future lives, just as your past lives have shaped this one."

Killian nodded, his heart filled with gratitude for the wisdom of the wise souls and the gift of exploring his past lives through dreams. With newfound clarity, he was ready to weave the threads of his destiny into a magnificent tapestry that spanned both the human and spiritual worlds.

The sun had risen higher into the sky, casting golden rays upon Killian's bedroom. He sat at the edge of his bed, toes resting on the smooth wooden floorboards that held the warmth of the sunlight. Around him, the room seemed to hum with an energy he hadn't noticed before, as if his newfound understanding of human consciousness had awakened him to the subtle vibrations of life.

"Consciousness is like a river," Silas explained in gentle tones, his delicate presence hovering just above the floor. "It flows through all living beings, connecting them to one another and to the larger web of existence."

"Think of your own consciousness as a droplet in that vast river," Aria added. "Your past lives are like streams that have merged together, creating who you are now."

Killian closed his eyes, trying to envision the metaphor. The idea was beautiful yet complex, and he struggled to grasp the full implications of it. His mind raced with questions about the nature of reality and the role of human consciousness in the grand scheme of things.

"Remember," Silas said softly, sensing his confusion, "the journey toward understanding is often more important than the destination. It is through exploration and contemplation that we grow."

"True wisdom comes from within," Aria agreed. "We can guide you, but ultimately, you must find the answers for yourself."

Killian nodded, feeling both challenged and encouraged by their words. As he pondered the insights he had gained from the wise souls, he began to realize that the decision he needed to make about his future was not something that could be rushed or forced. It required deep reflection and a connection to the core of his being.

"Take your time, Killian," Silas urged, his voice like a soothing balm on his troubled thoughts. "Listen to the whispers of your heart, and let them guide you."

"Trust yourself," Aria added, her eyes shining with gentle confidence. "You have the wisdom of countless lifetimes within you."

Killian breathed deeply, allowing their words to wash over him. He felt a sense of calm settle in his chest, and he understood that the key to reconciling his two lives lay not in choosing one over the other but in embracing both as part of his soul's journey.

"Thank you," he said softly, his voice thick with emotion. "Your guidance has been invaluable."

"Remember, we are always here for you, Killian," Silas assured him. "Simply call upon us when you need our wisdom."

"Indeed," Aria agreed. "Our souls are intertwined, just as all things in this universe are connected."

With a renewed sense of purpose, Killian stood up from the edge of the bed and gazed out the window at the sunlit world beyond. He knew that the path ahead would be filled with challenges and moments of doubt, but he also knew that he now had the tools to navigate them.

"Whatever my future holds," he whispered to himself, "I am ready to face it with courage, wisdom, and an open heart."

Killian stepped into the sunlit garden, where the vibrant colors of the flowers seemed to have gained a new depth and clarity. He felt the warmth of the sunlight on his face, the gentle breeze stirring the leaves around him, and the soft earth beneath his feet. The colors, sounds, and scents of the world appeared richer than ever before, as if he was experiencing them for the first time.

"Killian?" Lindsay's voice called out to him from the other side of the garden, her figure framed by the lush foliage.

"Over here," he replied, raising a hand in greeting. As she approached, Killian couldn't help but marvel at the love that swelled within him. Lindsay had been his constant companion through many lifetimes, and their connection transcended the boundaries of the physical world.

"Are you feeling better?" Lindsay asked with genuine concern, her eyes searching his face for any signs of distress.

"Much better," Killian replied, smiling warmly at her. "I've received guidance from Silas and Aria, and I've realized that my two lives aren't separate entities but part of a larger whole."

Lindsay's face lit up with relief and understanding. "That's wonderful news, Killian. So what are your plans for the future?"

"First and foremost, I want to deepen our relationship," Killian said sincerely, taking Lindsay's hands in his own. "We're connected not just through this life but through all our past lives as well. I want to explore that connection further and learn from our shared experiences."

"Would that involve the dream state you mentioned earlier?" Lindsay inquired, curiosity sparkling in her eyes.

"Exactly," Killian confirmed. "Together, we can use the dream state to explore our past lives, gain insight into our true selves, and learn how to navigate the challenges we face in this life."

"Sounds like quite the adventure," Lindsay mused, a smile tugging at the corners of her lips.

"Indeed, it will be," Killian agreed. "And beyond that, I'll be using my newfound knowledge to help others. There's so much wisdom and understanding within each of us, just waiting to be discovered. I want to share that with the world."

"Your selflessness has always been one of your most admirable qualities," Lindsay said softly, her eyes shimmering with pride.

"Thank you, Lindsay," Killian whispered, touched by her words. "It's because of you that I've come this far."

As they stood in the garden, hands entwined, Killian felt a sense of peace settle over him like a gentle embrace. He knew that his journey would be filled with challenges, but with Lindsay by his side and the guidance of the wise souls who had shown him the way, he was prepared to face whatever the future held.

In that moment, Killian understood that his experiences were a microcosm of the larger themes of life, love, loss, growth, and rebirth. The connections he forged both in the physical and spiritual realms would serve as a testament to the resilience and beauty of the human spirit. For it was through these bonds that the true essence of being human could be discovered, elevating one's consciousness to new heights and transcending the boundaries of time and space. And in the end, that was what mattered most.

Chapter 11

The Choice

The dimly lit living room of the Flaherty home was filled with an air of melancholy as Jennifer, Casey, Joe, and Hannah sat on their white linen couch. The shadows cast by the flickering candlelight on their faces seemed to reflect the heavy weight that had been burdening them for the past eight months.

"Eight months," Jennifer whispered, her voice quivering as she clutched a steaming mug of chamomile tea between her hands. "Eight months since Dad slipped into that coma, and not a single sign of him waking up."

Joe's jaw tightened, and he looked down at his clenched fists, which were resting on his knees. His usual cool composure was betrayed by the tremble in his hands as he tried to hold back tears. "It's just…it's just so hard, you know? Not knowing if he'll ever be himself again, if he'll ever come back to us."

Hannah's eyes brimmed with unshed tears as she tried to console her brother. Her own heartache was evident in the way her shoulders shook and the tremor in her voice as she spoke. "I know, Joe. I miss Dad too. Every day, it feels like there's this gaping hole in our lives where he used to be."

Casey, usually the optimist of the family, struggled to find any silver lining in the situation. He stared blankly at the oriental rug, tracing the patterns in his head, feeling the emptiness gnaw at his insides. "We all miss him, more than words can describe. This house...it's just not the same without him."

As the family exchanged their sorrows and fears, the absence of Killian was palpable in every corner of the room—the empty armchair where he used to sit and read his fake news on his mobile phone, the cold fireplace that he would light every evening, and the silent speaker that once filled the room with his favorite music. The bittersweet memories of him permeated the very air they breathed, making their hearts ache even more.

"Every night, I lie awake in our bed and wish he was lying next to me," Jennifer confessed, tears streaming down her cheeks as she stared into the flickering candle flame. "But then I remember the man lying in that hospital bed, trapped in his own mind, and it's like a knife twisting in my heart."

Joe wiped his eyes with the back of his hand, his voice cracking as he tried to hold back the tide of emotions threatening to overwhelm him. "I just can't believe this is happening to us, to Dad. He's the strongest person I know, and seeing him like this... it's unbearable."

Hannah reached out and grasped her mother's hand, her own fingers trembling with the effort to provide comfort. "We have to stay strong for Dad and for each other. That's what he would want for us."

As the family sat together, united in their grief, the silence that settled over them seemed to echo the void left by Killian's absence, filling the room with an oppressive weight that threatened to suffocate them all.

Jennifer's gaze drifted to the calendar pinned on the wall, each square filled with scribbled appointments and reminders. Since Killian's coma began, she had found solace in her weekly visits to his bedside. The familiar rhythm of her footsteps echoed through the hospital corridors, a soothing metronome that marked each passing week.

"Every time I see him, I whisper in his ear that we love him and that we're waiting for him," Jennifer said softly, her words barely a breath as they hung in the air. "I hold his hand and tell him about our days, hoping he can hear me, even just a little."

Casey's eyes sparkled with determination, a flicker of hope burning brightly in their depths. "I read somewhere that people in comas can sometimes still sense things happening around them," he mused, his voice steady and reassuring. "There are stories of people waking up after months or even years, remembering conversations they overheard while unconscious."

"Maybe Dad is just taking his time, trying to find his way back to us," Casey continued, his optimism a beacon for the family in their darkest moments. "One day, he'll open his eyes, and everything will be like it was before."

The image of Killian smiling, vibrant and full of life, danced in front of Jennifer's eyes, tantalizingly close yet painfully out of reach. She squeezed Hannah's hand, drawing strength from her daughter's unwavering support. "We have to believe that he's still in there, fighting to come back to us," she whispered, more to herself than anyone else.

As if summoned by their collective will, a sudden gust of wind rustled the curtains, carrying with it the scent of rain and the promise of renewal. The fragile coil of hope spun around Jennifer's heart, each beat a quiet prayer for Killian's return.

"Sometimes, when I close my eyes, I can feel his presence," she whispered, her voice soft and vulnerable. "As if he's standing right beside me, watching over us."

"Maybe he is, Mom," Casey said gently, his optimism infectious. "Maybe he's just waiting for the right moment to come back to us, stronger than ever."

Jennifer nodded, a determined spark igniting within her. "We'll be there for him, every step of the way," she vowed, her voice steady with conviction. "Together, we'll help him find his way home."

The sun dipped below the horizon, casting an eerie glow over the Flaherty household. Shadows danced across the walls as Joe paced the living room, his movements jagged and frantic like a caged animal. He could feel the storm brewing within him, threatening to break free and drench everything in its path.

"Mom," he finally said, his voice tight with barely restrained frustration. "We can't just give up on him. Pulling the plug…it's like we're killing him ourselves."

Jennifer stood near the window, her gaze fixed on the failing light outside. Her expression betrayed her inner turmoil, but she refused to let her resolve waver. She knew that making these difficult decisions was part of her duty to her family, and she would not back down.

"Joe, I don't want this any more than you do," she replied, her voice trembling ever so slightly. "But it's been eight months, and there's been no sign of improvement. We must face the reality of our situation. It has become a painful routine. Dad's not gone, but he is not with us either."

Hannah sat on the edge of the couch, her hands clutched tightly together as if they were the only things holding her together. The weight of her sadness pressed heavily upon her chest, suffocating her with the unbearable knowledge that she might lose her father forever. She stared at the worn oriental rug, unable to meet her mom or brother's eyes and see the pain mirrored in their gazes.

"Is there really nothing else we can do?" Hannah asked, her voice barely audible. "There must be some other option, some other treatment we haven't tried yet."

Joe stopped pacing and looked at his sister, desperation etched into the lines on his face. "That's what I keep saying, Hannah. We can't just give up on him. There has to be something we can do."

"Joe." Jennifer sighed, turning away from the window to face her son. "I've spoken with the doctors and explored every option they've presented us. Dad's been through countless tests, treatments, and therapies…and nothing has worked."

"Maybe we need to give it more time," Joe insisted, clenching his fists at his sides. "What if he's just on the brink of a breakthrough? What if we're only days away from him waking up?"

"Or what if we're holding onto false hope?" Jennifer countered, a tear escaping her eye and tracing a shimmering path down her cheek. "It's been eight months, Joe, eight months of watching our family suffer, of seeing my children struggle with the pain of losing their father. How much longer can we keep doing this?"

Hannah listened to Jennifer and Joe's heated exchange, feeling as if a chasm was growing between them, threatening to swallow her whole. She wanted to believe that her father could recover, but she also understood her mother's desire to end their collective suffering.

"Mom, Joe, please," Hannah whispered, her voice cracking. "Arguing won't help. We need to make this decision together, as a family."

A heavy silence descended upon the room, broken only by the distant rumble of thunder. The storm outside mirrored the emotional storm within the Flaherty household, the tension so thick it could be cut with a knife.

"All right, Hannah," Jennifer conceded, wiping away her tears. "We'll discuss this further, weigh all our options, and make the best decision for Dad and our family."

Joe nodded in agreement, the frustration still simmering beneath the surface but the love for his mom and siblings overpowering it. They would face this storm together, united by their love for Killian and their determination to do right by him. And as the rain began to fall outside, the Flaherty family braced themselves for the difficult journey ahead.

A single tear slid down the rain-streaked windowpane, mirroring the sadness that clung to the Flaherty family like a heavy fog. Inside the living room, Jennifer sat with her hands clasped tightly in her lap, her knuckles turning white from the pressure. Joe paced back and forth, his eyes darting between his mom and sister, searching for answers in their anguished faces. Hannah stared at a photograph of happier times, her father's smile a mere memory now.

"Eight months," Jennifer whispered, her voice barely audible over the soft patter of raindrops on the roof. "I can't believe it's been eight months since Killian slipped away from us."

"His body is here, but he's not," Joe added solemnly, stopping his pacing to look out the window at the gray sky. "It's like living in limbo, waiting for something to change."

Hannah blinked away her tears, clutching the photograph to her chest. "Every time the phone rings, I hope it's the hospital telling us he's woken up and that our lives can go back to normal. But it never is."

The family shared a somber silence, each lost in memories of the man who had once filled their home with laughter and love. The routine of visiting the hospital, holding Killian's lifeless hand, and praying for a miracle had become a part of their lives, a cruel reminder that their husband and father was neither truly with them nor completely gone.

"Enough," Jennifer said suddenly, her voice firm yet gentle. "We need to decide what's best for Dad. We owe him that much."

"Mom's right," Joe agreed, his frustration giving way to determination. "Let's go to the hospital. Together."

With a collective deep breath, the Flaherty family stood, bracing themselves for the most difficult decision they had ever faced. As they stepped outside into the storm, the rain seemed to cleanse them of their uncertainties. They walked side by side, a united front against the cruel hand fate had dealt them. And as they drove toward the hospital, it felt as though the weight of their grief was momentarily lifted, replaced by a quiet, steely resolve. No matter what lay ahead, they would face it together, guided by love and the memory of the man who had brought them all so much joy.

The tension in Killian's hospital room was palpable as family and friends gathered, their expressions a mix of worry, hope, and uncertainty. As Jennifer and her children entered the room, she stood by Killian's bedside, her hands wringing a tissue as she occasionally wiped away tears. Her eyes were red-rimmed and exhausted, yet she held herself with a quiet strength that spoke volumes.

Across the room, Killian's parents huddled together, whispering in hushed tones, while his friend, Brian, stood near the door, arms crossed, his face etched with concern. Two lawyers, one representing the hospital and the other representing Killian's family, looked over documents, occasionally glancing up at the strained faces around them.

*****

The sterile scent of antiseptic filled Killian's nostrils as he lay in the hospital bed, in his mind his eyes flickering open to take in the room around him but not visible to those in the room. The dull hum of machines and the rhythmic beeping of the heart monitor filled his ears, grounding him in the reality of his situation. The walls were an uninspired off-white, the paint chipped in places, revealing a darker color beneath. As his mind roamed over the room, it settled on the various medical equipment that surrounded him, an IV pole with bags of fluids and medications, the monitor displaying his vital signs, and the ventilator that breathed for him.

His thoughts were racing as he tried to make sense of what was happening. He could feel the weight of the decision he had to make, pressing down on him like a crushing force, suffocating him.

Dr. Cohen entered the room and stepped forward, flipping through pages on a clipboard before addressing the room. "As you know," he began, his voice steady but shaded with empathy, "Jennifer and I discussed the possibility of removing Killian's life support. We understand this is an incredibly difficult decision, and we want to make sure everyone is fully informed before any choices are made."

The room seemed to collectively hold its breath, each person silently grappling with their own thoughts and emotions. Killian's heart ached as he watched them, his mind churning with memories and possibilities. The decision he had to make felt impossible, like choosing between the very air he breathed or the blood that flowed through his veins.

With every beat of his heart, the pressure mounted. The lives and relationships at stake weighed heavily on him, and yet he knew the choice was his alone to make. And so in the dimly lit hospital room, surrounded by the ones he loved most, Killian prepared to face the most challenging decision of his life.

Killian's consciousness teetered on the edge of two very different worlds, his thoughts swirling as if caught in the eye of a storm. The choice before him was clear: remain with Lindsay but risk losing his connection as his consciousness searched for a new earthly vessel or return to his present life with Jennifer and their children with the hope that he could return to Lindsay in his dreams. But clarity did little to ease the torrent of emotions that threatened to engulf him.

"Lindsay," he whispered, her name a balm to his heartache. He remembered the way her laughter had filled their small cottage, like the scent of jasmine on a warm summer night. He recalled how she'd looked at him with eyes that held both the depths of the ocean and the promise of a thousand sunsets. In her arms, he'd known what it meant to be alive, truly alive, for the first time in his life.

"Killian, stay." The memory of her voice washed over him, soothing yet imploring. They'd danced beneath the stars until the world around them faded away, leaving only the rhythm of their hearts and the warmth of their love. "You belong here, with me."

But the memory of Lindsay soon began to blur, replaced by the image of Jennifer's face, her smile, a beacon of light guiding him home through the fog of his pain. The sound of their children's laughter echoed in his ears, a melody more beautiful than any symphony. Their life together may have been routine, but it was the life they had built with love and dedication.

"Please come back to us, Killian." Jennifer's plea resonated within him, an anchor tethering him to the present. "We need you. I need you."

"Choose, Killian," the voices whispered, each one pulling him in opposite directions, stretching him thin like a fraying rope. "Choose."

He closed his eyes, letting the memories flood his senses. There was Lindsay, twirling beneath a moonlit sky, her laughter as bubbly as champagne. And then there was Jennifer, cradling their newborn child in her arms, exhaustion and love mingling on her face.

"Choose," Silas's voice insisted, growing louder, more insistent. "Choose!"

"Enough!" Killian cried out, his voice cracking under the weight of the decision. He saw himself standing at a fork in the road, the paths before him disappearing into the distance. On one side, the road led back to Lindsay, their love an unending symphony and their passion a fire that would never die. On the other, the path wound through the life he shared with Jennifer, the quiet moments of happiness, and the laughter of their children echoing through the air.

"Choose!" The voices thundered like a storm, threatening to shatter his very soul.

"Please help me, Silas," he whispered, his voice barely audible above the deafening noise. As the moment stretched on, Killian's heart remained torn between two lives, two loves, and the daunting task of choosing just one.

Killian's heart ached as he stood, teetering on the edge of an abyss. On one side, there was Lindsay, their love a raging tempest that had consumed him whole. He could feel the warmth of her hand in his, the scent of her perfume as they danced through moonlit gardens, and the taste of her lips after a stolen kiss.

"Choose me," she whispered, a faint echo of a memory that stirred within him like a half-forgotten dream. "Choose us."

On the other side of the chasm, there was Jennifer, gentle, steadfast, and unwavering. He recalled the softness of her laughter as they watched their children play in the park, the tender way she nurtured them through every scrape and bruise, and the fierce love that bound them together through the trials of life.

"Choose our family," she implored, her voice laced with hope and desperation. "Choose our future."

"Please stop," Killian begged, overwhelmed by the weight of the decision before him. It felt as though his very soul was being torn apart, each life beckoning to him like sirens' songs, each moment more precious than the last.

"Choose!" the voices insisted, relentless in their pursuit. "Choose!"

"Enough!" he cried out, his voice raw and broken. He clenched his fists, feeling as if he were being pulled apart by invisible hands, his mind caught in a viselike grip. "I can't…I can't—"

"Killian," both women called out, their voices entwining like ivy, begging for his decision.

"Jennifer..." Killian breathed, leaning toward the life he had built with her. But then, a gust of wind carried Lindsay's laughter through the air, and he wavered, drawn back to the woman who had ignited his soul like no other.

"Choose!" the voices roared, an unstoppable force threatening to consume him whole.

"Let me go," Killian whispered, surrendering to the deafening sounds. And as he did, the world around him crumbled, collapsing in on itself like a dying star. He felt the cold embrace of death, a shroud that threatened to suffocate him as it wove its coil through his very being.

"Choose!" The voices demanded one final time, their voices thunderous, echoing through the void.

"Please..." he choked out, tears streaming down his face, his resolve crumbling under the weight of the decision. "Please..."

"Choose!" They screamed, and as they did, Killian felt himself plummeting toward the abyss, the darkness swallowing him whole as he grappled with the impossibility of his choice.

"Killian, you know I love you," she whispered, her voice cracking under the weight of her words. "But we need to move forward. It's been eight long months, and it's time for us to heal. The kids need their father, but they also need stability."

"Please, Dad," Killian's daughter, Hannah, added, her innocent eyes brimming with tears. "We miss you so much. We just want you back with us."

"Are you kidding me, Killian? Your family needs you," urged his best friend, Brian, giving him a supportive pat on the shoulder. "You've built a life with them, and it's a life worth fighting for."

But amid the chorus of voices urging him to choose his present life, one familiar voice cut through the chatter, Lindsay's. As if carried by the wind, her voice reached him from across the void.

"Killian, remember the laughter? The joy we shared?" Her voice was soft, a gentle reminder of the passion that had once consumed them. "Our love was like fire…can you really let that go?"

His heart wrenched at her voice, torn between the blissful memories they'd shared and the life he'd built with Jennifer and their children. He closed his eyes, desperately trying to silence the storm raging inside him.

"Killian, please," Jennifer implored, her eyes glistening with unshed tears. "I know how much your past lives mean to you, but we have a family now. We have responsibilities. Our love may not be as wild and untamed as what you had in your other lives, but it's strong, and it's real."

"Please, Killian," Hannah whispered again, her small hands grasping his tightly. "We need you here with us. We can't lose you."

The weight of their words bore down on him, threatening to crush him beneath the magnitude of his decision. It was a choice between the fierce love and passion he'd experienced with Lindsay and the steady warmth and devotion that had grown with Jennifer and their children.

Killian's heart ached as he grappled with the impossible decision before him. He retreated into his mind, seeking solace in memories of both lives that had shaped him. The hospital room seemed to fade away, replaced by vivid scenes from his past.

He found himself walking hand in hand with Lindsay through a sunlit meadow, wildflowers dancing in the breeze around them. Their laughter rang out like music, pure and unrestrained. In her eyes, he saw the spark that had ignited their passionate love affairs across timelines. It was a time when life felt limitless—an era of reckless abandon and breathtaking adventure.

"Remember this, Killian?" Lindsay whispered, her voice echoing through his mind. "We were free. We soared together. Can you really let go of what we had?"

Yet just as quickly as it appeared, the meadow dissolved, and Killian found himself standing in the cozy living room of his home with Jennifer. They were surrounded by their children, faces glowing in the warm light of the fireplace. The soothing scent of freshly baked cookies filled the air, mingling with the familiar smell of well-worn books lining the shelves. Killian watched as Jennifer read to their youngest son, her gentle voice lulling him to sleep.

"Look at what we've built together," Jennifer entreated softly. "We have a family, Killian, a life full of love and support. Isn't that worth fighting for?"

The two scenes flickered back and forth, struggling for dominance in Killian's mind. Each memory tugged at his heart, pulling him in opposite directions. He could feel the warmth of Lindsay's touch and the electric current that surged between them whenever they locked eyes but also the comforting weight of Jennifer's hand on his shoulder and the steady reassurance in her gaze.

As the hospital room began to materialize once more, Killian strained to focus on the sensory details around him, hoping they could anchor him to the present. The sterile scent of antiseptic filled his nostrils, while the persistent beeping of the machines provided a rhythmic backdrop to his thoughts. The soft swish of fabric against fabric told him that Jennifer and Lindsay were still by his side, each desperate for him to choose.

"Dad." Hannah's voice quivered, but her determination was palpable. "We're here for you. We'll always be here, no matter what."

The simple truth in her words resonated within him, echoing through the chambers of his heart. He knew he had to make a decision—one life had to be relinquished to fully embrace the other. It was a choice he couldn't defer any longer.

With a deep breath, Killian gathered the threads of his life, weaving together the patchwork of memories and emotions that had led him to this moment. His fingers trembled as they reached out to grasp the delicate strands, pulling them tight with the weight of his decision.

The hospital room seemed to hold its breath as Killian tightened his grip on the threads of his two lives. He could feel the weight of the decision bearing down on him, threatening to crush him beneath its enormity. A single tear rolled down his cheek, a testament to the emotional turmoil that churned within him.

"Please," Jennifer whispered, her voice hoarse from hours of tense silence. "I know this is hard, but you have to choose. We can't do this for you."

"Killian, don't forget what we had," Lindsay implored, her eyes pleading and glistening with unshed tears. "You were my everything."

"But he's our everything now," Hannah chimed in, her young voice wavering yet steadfast in her conviction. "Dad…please, we need you."

A moment of clarity pierced through the fog of Killian's mind, bringing with it an overwhelming sense of purpose. His gaze traveled between Jennifer and Lindsay, etching their faces into his memory. Then, finally, he made his choice.

"Jennifer," he breathed, releasing one set of threads as the other solidified in his grasp. "I choose you. I choose our family."

Chapter 12

Return to the Nest

Killian's world became a whirlwind of colors, emotions, and sensations. He felt as if he were caught in a vortex, spinning faster and faster, until he could no longer discern the difference between dreams and reality. In the eye of this storm, two powerful forces tugged at his heart: Jennifer, his beloved wife on his earthly plane, and Lindsay, the delicate woman who inhabited another realm entirely and who has been his soulmate across multiple timelines.

"Killian," Lindsay whispered into the chaos, her hair billowing like sheets drying on a clothesline in a gentle breeze. Her eyes held a wisdom that pierced through the confusion, beckoning him toward her embrace. For a moment, Killian was tempted to abandon himself to the solace of her arms, but something deep within him resisted.

"Jennifer," he whispered, the name escaping his lips like a lifeline. The mere thought of his wife fortified his resolve, reminding him of the life they had built together, their children, and the commitment he had sworn to uphold. Killian's practical mind seized this anchor, forcing him to resist the allure of Lindsay's presence. It was as if an invisible tether yanked him back from the edge of oblivion.

As Killian's consciousness pulled away from Lindsay, he felt a sudden jolt in his physical body. A faint gasp echoed around the sterile room, a sound that did not go unnoticed by the group of loved ones gathered at his bedside.

"Did you see that?" Jennifer whispered, her voice trembling with a mixture of excitement and caution. She gently grasped Killian's hand, her strong will pulling him to return to her side.

"His eyelids fluttered," Hannah confirmed, her eyes wide with hope.

"Everyone, step back for a moment," Dr. Cohen instructed, his tone authoritative but laced with anticipation. They all complied, watching intently as he flashed a penlight into Killian's eyes, searching for any sign of his return.

"Come on, Dad," Joe whispered under his breath, fists clenched at his sides. The air in the room was thick with a cocktail of hope, fear, and anticipation.

"Jennifer," Killian's voice echoed once more in the whirlwind of sensations, growing stronger as his consciousness tore itself away from Lindsay's grasp. He knew that he must return to his wife, to live the life they had forged together. Yet even as he made this decision, a part of him mourned the loss of the connection he had shared with Lindsay.

With a sudden gasp, Killian's body jolted back to life. Killian's eyes fluttered open, the sterile scent of the hospital room filling his nostrils as he slowly regained consciousness. His body felt weak and heavy like a sack of stones, and a dull ache throbbed in the back of his skull. The steady beeping of the heart monitor provided a rhythmic anchor to reality. Killian tried to move, but it was as if his limbs were bound by invisible chains.

"Killian!" Jennifer exclaimed softly, her voice wavering between elation and disbelief. She moved closer to him, her hand reaching out to brush his clammy forehead tenderly. "You're back."

"Jen…" Killian whispered, the effort it took to form the words leaving him breathless. He wanted to tell her everything, about the world he had just left, and the woman who had haunted his dreams. But he couldn't, not yet.

"Take your time," Jennifer urged, her eyes searching his face for any sign of discomfort or pain. "We're all here for you." Their children, still bearing traces of their youthful innocence, nodded in agreement, their eyes glistening with unshed tears.

"Thank you," Killian managed to whisper before his gaze drifted to the window, where the last light of the setting sun cast an otherworldly glow over the room. It reminded him of Lindsay, and a pang of longing twisted in his chest.

"Doctor, when can we take him home?" Jennifer asked, her voice betraying the desperation she felt, to return to normalcy.

"Let's give him some time to regain his strength," the doctor replied cautiously, scribbling notes on his chart. "But I'm now optimistic about his recovery."

Killian's heart swelled at the thought of returning to the life he had built with Jennifer, the cozy home, the laughter of their children, and the warmth of her embrace. And yet he couldn't help but feel a twinge of guilt for the part of him that longed to see Lindsay again.

As Jennifer and the children chatted excitedly about his progress, Killian allowed himself to sink into the soft folds of the hospital bed, his thoughts adrift between two worlds. He knew that he could not have both lives, one where he was a devoted husband and father and another where he explored the depths of a mystical connection with Lindsay.

"Killian," Jennifer whispered as she leaned in close, her lips brushing against his ear. "We'll get through this together. I promise."

His heart ached at her unwavering love and loyalty, knowing that he did not deserve it. But despite the turmoil swirling within him, Killian vowed to honor the life he had built with Jennifer, even if it meant burying the memory of Lindsay deep within the recesses of his soul.

"Thank you," he whispered, his voice barely audible. And with those words, Killian began his journey back into the world, determined to find a balance between the love he bore for his family and the ghost of a woman who had stolen his heart.

"Mr. Flaherty?" A voice pierced through the fog in his mind. "Can you hear me?"

Killian turned his head, wincing at the stiffness in his neck. A woman in scrubs stood by his bed, her eyes filled with equal parts surprise and concern. "You've been in a coma for quite some time."

"Where am I?" Killian croaked, his throat raw and aching.

"You're at St. Mary's Hospital," she replied gently. "In the city."

His heart clenched as memories began to surface like boxes from a shipwreck. The peaceful coastal town he'd called home for so many years now felt like a distant dream, replaced by the cold, clinical reality of the hospital room. The only connection to the outside world came from the window beside his bed, revealing a sprawling city skyline where once there had been a vast expanse of ocean.

"City…" he whispered, the word feeling foreign on his tongue. The quiet life he'd known before, the one filled with love and laughter, seemed impossibly far away, swallowed by the concrete jungle that loomed just beyond the glass.

"Mr. Flaherty." Dr. Cohen's voice reverberated through the room. "We're glad to see you conscious again. How are you feeling?"

Killian didn't respond, his gaze locked on the window, as if willing the ocean to return. He could almost feel the sand beneath his feet and hear the gentle crashing of waves against the shore. It was Lindsay's laughter that echoed most clearly in his mind, her smile brighter than the sun on their shared beach strolls. They were inseparable, two souls fused by an unwavering love.

"Mr. Flaherty?" Dr. Cohen persisted, concern etching lines into his forehead. "Can you speak?"

"Where is she?" Killian finally rasped, the words barely audible. His heart ached for Lindsay and for the life they had built together. He longed for the weightlessness of their scuba diving adventures and the way the underwater world seemed to cradle them in its embrace.

"Who are you talking about?" the doctor asked, confusion clouding his features.

"Never mind." Killian sighed, defeated. The realization that he must face his real life with Jennifer weighed heavily upon him, smothering the remnants of his idyllic existence with Lindsay. He knew he couldn't avoid the truth forever, but the thought of leaving behind the woman who had captured his heart felt like a betrayal he couldn't bear.

"Mr. Flaherty, it's important for your recovery that you communicate with us," Dr. Cohen urged, "we're here to help."

"Leave me alone," Killian muttered, turning away from Dr. Cohen. He couldn't bring himself to accept their assistance, knowing it would only push him further from the life he must now work to forget.

"All right, I'll give you some time," Dr. Cohen conceded, "but remember, we're here when you need us."

As the door clicked shut behind the departing Dr. Cohen, Killian's thoughts swirled with the memories of Lindsay and the love they shared. His heart ached with conflict as he tried to reconcile the two lives that tugged at its seams.

The door creaked open, and the scent of Jennifer's perfume wafted into the room before she even crossed the threshold. Killian lay in bed and braced himself for the conversation that was sure to come.

"Killian," Jennifer said softly, her voice strained with emotion as she approached the bed. "You can't keep shutting everyone out. We're all worried about you."

Her words hung heavily in the air, and Killian couldn't help but compare them to the easy, carefree conversations he had shared with Lindsay. They used to laugh together like children, their voices mingling with the salty sea breeze. But now, his heart sank at the weight of this new reality.

"Look, I know it's difficult for you," Jennifer continued, her eyes glistening with unshed tears. "But you need to work with the doctors if you want to get better. You can't just give up."

"Give up?" Killian snapped, anger bubbling up within him as his thoughts spiraled back to his life with Lindsay. "You think I want to be here? Trapped in this godforsaken room, surrounded by machines and sterile walls?"

"I'm sorry, Killian," Jennifer whispered, her voice cracking. "I didn't mean it like that. I just…I don't want to lose you again."

"Neither do I," Killian thought, but his mind lingered on the woman he was also afraid of losing. The memory of Lindsay's sun-kissed skin and the warmth of her embrace still haunted him.

"Please," Jennifer implored, reaching out to grasp his hand. "You have to try. For us." Her hazel eyes were filled with concern and relief. She tenderly brushed a strand of hair from his forehead, her touch soft and comforting. "You've been in a coma for quite some time."

"J-Jennifer?" Killian croaked, his voice hoarse and raspy. He could see the worry etched on her face, the lines that had deepened over the weeks of his unconsciousness. It was then that memories from his past life surfaced, crashing into him like waves against jagged cliffs: the warm glow of laughter shared with Lindsay, the touch of her lips against his skin, and the bittersweet pain of their parting words.

"Killian? What's wrong?" Jennifer asked, noticing the flicker of confusion and longing that clouded his eyes.

"Nothing," he whispered, forcing a smile onto his lips. "Just…memories from before." He didn't want to burden her with his conflicted emotions, not when she already had so much to bear. As much as he cherished the life he'd built with Jennifer and their children, the lingering love he still harbored for Lindsay gnawed at him, threatening to unravel the fragile threads of his present existence.

"Are you sure?" Jennifer pressed gently, sensing there was more to his response than he was willing to share. He looked away, unable to meet her gaze, and for a moment, silence settled heavily between them.

"Jennifer," he began hesitantly, his voice barely above a whisper. "What if…what if I told you that I remember things from before the coma? Things that I can't explain?"

"Like what?" she asked cautiously, her eyes narrowing with concern.

"Memories," Killian replied, swallowing hard. "Memories of a life I lived before this one."

"Killian, I don't understand," Jennifer whispered, her brow furrowed in confusion. "What are you trying to say?"

"Jennifer, I…" He trailed off, unsure of how to express the tangled web of emotions that threatened to overwhelm him. The memories of Lindsay seemed so vivid, almost tangible; their love felt like it had been etched into the very fabric of his soul.

"Killian, it's okay," Jennifer said softly, placing a reassuring hand on his arm. "Whatever you're going through, we'll figure it out together. You don't have to carry this burden alone." Her words were soothing, a balm to his frayed nerves, but they did little to limit the turmoil brewing within him.

As much as Killian longed to be present in his renewed life with Jennifer and their children, the ghost of his past love haunted him, a specter that refused to be banished. He was torn between two worlds, the life he'd once known with Lindsay and the one he now shared with Jennifer. And as he lay there, trapped within his own thoughts, he couldn't help but wonder if he would ever find peace amidst the chaos of his own conflicting emotions.

As Killian enjoyed his first week back home from the hospital, a gust of wind rustled through the leaves of a nearby tree as Killian sat on the porch, watching his children play in the yard. The sunlight danced on their faces, and he marveled at the sight before him, the reflection of Jennifer's love manifested in their bright eyes and playful laughter. He felt a surge of warmth and protectiveness toward them, fueled by an intense desire to make things work with this family that had been gifted to him.

"Hey, Killian," Jennifer called out as she joined him on the porch, handing him a glass of iced tea. "The kids are having a blast. Are you okay?" she asked, concern etched across her face.

He looked into her eyes, seeing the worry that hid behind her smile. "I'm trying, Jennifer. I want to be there for you and the kids. It's just…" His voice trailed off; the words caught in his throat like a fishhook.

Jennifer placed a reassuring hand on his knee. "We'll take it one day at a time," she said softly, encouraging him to let go of the past.

As he sipped his tea, the taste of lemon and mint mingling on his tongue, Killian was suddenly pulled back into a memory of Lindsay. They were sitting in their small cottage, laughing over a shared cup of hot chocolate. The air was thick with steam from the simmering pot on the stove, the windows fogged up from the heat.

"Killian," Lindsay whispered, wiping a smudge of whipped cream from his lips. "Promise me we'll always be together, no matter what."

"I promise," he had replied, his heart swelling with love for the woman who had captured his soul.

But fate had other plans. In a cruel twist of events, they found themselves drifting apart, their once passionate love now reduced to a pile of cold ashes. The last conversation they had was one filled with tears and heartache, as they acknowledged the end of their journey together.

"Killian." Lindsay sobbed, her voice barely audible. "I can't do this anymore. I love you, but we both know it's not enough to save us."

"Lindsay!" Killian shouted with strong yet passionate plea. "My consciousness needs an earthly body to survive, which is available to me in my life with Jennifer. I know our passion has survived across multiple timelines and our souls are connected at levels beyond comprehension, but a complete life is more than just passion; it is the life you build with loved ones that matters most. I know you and I will find each other again somehow, somewhere, and I look forward to our reunion; however, for now in my current life, I chose to build upon my love for Jennifer and my family because of the strong bond as a family that is just beginning to blossom. They are as much a part of my timeline as you and I, and I need to build upon that to become a better husband, father, and friend to those I cherish."

"Goodbye for now, my love," he whispered, a single tear rolling down his cheek as he kissed her for the last time.

Back in the present, Killian shook off the memory, focusing on the sound of his children's laughter echoing through the yard. He knew that he couldn't change the past, nor could he forget the love he once shared with Lindsay. But he also recognized the love that now surrounded him; the love of a woman who stood by his side, even in the darkest of times; and the love of the children who called him "Dad" with such adoration.

"Jennifer," he said, turning toward her with renewed determination. "Thank you for being here with me. I promise to cherish our family and the love that binds us together."

"Killian, I know your heart is torn, but it's big enough to hold both the past and the present," Jennifer replied, her eyes glistening with unshed tears. "We'll make it work, together."

As they embraced, the sun dipped below the horizon, painting the sky with hues of pink and gold. In that moment, Killian resolved to strive for a balance between the love he felt for both Lindsay and Jennifer, knowing that each had shaped his life in ways that defied explanation. With that resolution came an understanding that he could find peace amidst the chaos of his own emotions, so long as he held onto the love that now anchored him to this world.

As Killian lay in bed that night, he found himself unable to sleep. The room was shrouded in darkness, moonlight filtering through the curtains and casting eerie shadows on the walls. His mind was a whirlwind of conflicting emotions, making his chest ache with the weight of them. He knew he loved Jennifer and their children deeply, but he couldn't deny that Lindsay still held a piece of his heart.

"Jennifer," Killian whispered into the night, as though speaking her name would somehow help him untangle the knots in his soul. "Jennifer—"

"Killian? Are you awake?" Jennifer's sleepy voice floated from beside him, and he realized she was still there, curled up next to him under the heavy weight of the blankets.

"Sorry," he whispered. "I didn't mean to wake you."

"Is something bothering you?" Jennifer asked, turning to face him. Her voice was full of concern, and he knew that she could sense his turmoil even in the darkness.

"Jennifer, I love our life together, and I cherish what we have," Killian began hesitantly. "But I can't seem to shake the memories of my past lives with Lindsay. It's like she's…haunting me."

"Killian, it's okay to feel those emotions," Jennifer replied softly, touching his arm reassuringly. "You spent lifetimes with her, and your memories of those times are a part of who you are now. It doesn't mean you love me or our children any less."

"Thank you for understanding," Killian said, his voice cracking. "I just want to be the best husband and father I can be, and sometimes, I worry that my past is holding me back."

"Your past has shaped you, Killian, but it doesn't define you," Jennifer reassured him. "We'll work through this together. You don't need to carry this burden alone."

"Thank you, Jennifer. I don't know what I'd do without you," Killian whispered, pulling her close and feeling her warmth seep into him.

"Always," she whispered against his chest.

The next day, as Killian watched their children play in the park, he couldn't help but marvel at the love that surrounded him. The laughter of his sons, Casey and Joe, rang through the air as they played football, while his daughter, Hannah, clung to his leg with a giggle, her cheeks flushed with delight.

"Dad, come throw the football for us," Joe called out excitedly, waving for him to join in the fun.

"All right, buddy! Let's play tag football together," Killian replied, scooping up Hannah and joining the boys.

As he immersed himself in the joy of the moment, Killian realized that although Lindsay would always be a part of him, it was Jennifer and their children who filled his heart now. They were his anchor in the storm of emotions that threatened to drown him, and with them by his side, he knew he could find peace amidst the tumultuous waves of his past.

"Jennifer," Killian said later that evening, as they sat on the porch watching the sun set. "I'm going to focus on our family and the love we share. Though Lindsay will always have a place in my heart, it's you, Casey, Joe, and Hannah who hold the keys to my happiness."

"Killian, that's all I've ever wanted," Jennifer replied, her eyes brimming with tears of relief. "Together, we'll create beautiful memories that will last a lifetime and many timelines of our own."

And as the sun dipped below the horizon, casting a golden glow over the world, Killian felt a sense of resolution wash over him. He knew that finding balance between the love for Lindsay and his love for Jennifer and their children would be a constant struggle, but he was determined to make it work. For the first time in what felt like ages, he could breathe freely, knowing that his heart was finally at peace.

Killian stood in the park, watching the leaves of the maple trees change color as autumn settled in. The crisp air reminded him of younger days, when life seemed simpler. He breathed it in deeply, feeling the weight of his conflicting emotions settle on his chest.

"Killian!" called a familiar voice from behind him. It was his older brother, Thomas, who had always been there for him in times of need. He approached Killian with a warm smile and a comforting pat on the back.

"Thomas," Killian replied, his voice strained. "I...I wanted to talk to you about something."

"Of course," Thomas said, concern evident in his eyes. They found an empty bench under a canopy of red and gold foliage and sat down together.

"Jennifer and I are doing well, but there's… there's still a part of me that can't let go of Lindsay," Killian admitted, his voice cracking slightly. His hands trembled in his lap, betraying the turmoil within.

"Killian," Thomas began gently, "it's not unusual to still have feelings for someone from your past, especially considering your history with Lindsay. But the important thing is to focus on what's in front of you now, Jennifer and the kids."

Killian looked into his brother's eyes, seeking reassurance. "I know, Thomas. I just…I feel so pulled in two different directions. How am I supposed to find balance?"

"Let me tell you something brother," Thomas said, leaning in closer. "Love isn't a finite resource. You don't have to choose one over the other. You can love them both, but in different ways. Just remember where your priorities lie."

As they spoke, a gentle breeze rustled through the leaves overhead, casting sunlight onto their faces. Killian felt a warmth spread through him, as if the words spoken by his brother were dissolving the cold knot of uncertainty in his heart.

"Thank you, Thomas," Killian said, his voice steadier now. "You're right. I need to focus on my present and my future with Jennifer and our children while still honoring the part of me that will always love Lindsay."

"Exactly." Thomas nodded, giving Killian's shoulder a reassuring squeeze. "Life is full of complexities, but it's how we navigate them that defines us."

Killian took a deep breath, letting the autumn air fill his lungs once more. He felt a renewed sense of resolve, knowing that he could find a way to reconcile his feelings for both women without sacrificing the life he had built with Jennifer and his children.

"Come on," Thomas said, standing up from the bench. "Let's go home with that beautiful family of yours."

Killian smiled, gratitude shining in his eyes as they walked together through the park, the fading sunlight casting long shadows behind them. And within him, a newfound understanding of love's many forms began to take root, guiding him toward a path of balance and peace.

Killian stood at the edge of his yard with the city skyline in the foreground and the varying sounds of the city seeming to mirror the ebb and flow of his emotions, caught between two worlds, the one he shared with Jennifer and their children and the one forever lost to him with Lindsay.

He closed his eyes, allowing the sounds and in that moment, Killian knew that he needed to make a decision, one that would impact not only his own life but also the lives of those he loved.

"Sometimes, the hardest decisions are the ones we have to make for the sake of others," he whispered to himself, remembering Thomas's words from their conversation in the park. His brother's advice had helped him see the situation more clearly, but now it was up to him to take action.

As Killian opened his eyes, he noticed a pigeon soaring overhead. It glided effortlessly on the currents of air, free from the constraints of land and the burden of choices. He envied its freedom, wishing that he too could simply spread his wings and find solace in the boundless sky above.

But he was not a bird, and he could not escape the weight of his decisions. Instead, he turned his attention to a small tree growing nearby, its roots clinging tenaciously to the rocky soil. Despite the harsh conditions, it had managed to survive and even thrive, adapting to its surroundings and finding a way to coexist alongside the elements that threatened to tear it apart.

"Balance," Killian whispered, recognizing the symbolism embodied by the tree. "That's what I need to find, a balance between the love I feel for Jennifer and our children and the love that remains for Lindsay."

A sudden gust of wind tugged at his hair as if to confirm his revelation. Killian took a deep breath, feeling the knot of uncertainty within him loosen ever so slightly. He knew that he could not change the past or erase the memories of his life with Lindsay, but he could choose how to move forward.

"Jennifer and the kids are my present, my future," he resolved, his voice strong and determined. "I will honor the love I felt for Lindsay and cherish the memories we shared, but I will also embrace the life I've built with Jennifer and make every effort to nurture our relationship and be there for my family."

With that decision made, Killian turned away from the street and started back up his driveway toward his front door. The sun dipped low in the sky, casting long shadows across the ground and bathing the world in a warm golden light. In that moment, Killian felt as though he had finally reached a measure of peace and a newfound understanding of the complexities of the universe and love and the delicate balance required to navigate them.

As he walked, the pigeon swooped down and landed on a nearby rooftop, its black eyes watching him intently. Killian couldn't help but smile, feeling as though the bird was offering its silent approval of his choice. With one final glance at the city skyline, he continued, his steps lighter and heart more at ease than they had been in a long time.

The following day, Killian awoke with a sense of purpose. Sunlight streamed through the curtains, casting a warm glow on the bedroom walls. The fresh scent of coffee wafted upstairs from the kitchen, drawing him out of bed and downstairs where Jennifer stood, her back to him as she busied herself with breakfast.

"Good morning," he said softly, wrapping his arms around her waist and pressing a gentle kiss to her neck.

"Morning," she replied, smiling as she turned in his embrace. "You seem…lighter today."

"I made a decision," Killian admitted, holding her gaze. "I want to be here, fully present with you and our children. I will always cherish the memories of my past life with Lindsay, but it's time to focus on our future together."

Jennifer studied his face for a moment before nodding, tears welling up in her eyes. "Thank you, Killian. That means everything to me."

As weeks went by, Killian took deliberate steps to strengthen his bond with Jennifer and their children. He attended football games, helped with homework, and planned date nights with his wife. Each action brought them closer and deepened their connection.

One evening, after the children were tucked into bed, Killian found Jennifer in the living room, sipping tea and reading a book. He sat beside her, pulling her into his arms.

"Jennifer, I love you, more than words can express," he whispered in her ear, feeling her body relax against him.

"I love you too," she whispered, setting her book aside and meeting his gaze.

"Let's take a trip, just the two of us," Killian suggested, excitement filling his voice. "We can leave the kids with my sister for a couple of days and reconnect as a couple."

"Sounds wonderful," Jennifer agreed, her eyes sparkling with anticipation.

As they planned their getaway, Killian felt his heart swell with love for his wife and family. He knew he had made the right choice, to honor his past but embrace his present and future with the ones who mattered most.

The day of their departure arrived as autumn leaves danced in the wind, their vibrant hues painting the world in warm colors. The crisp air seemed to hold a promise of renewal, reflecting Killian's own sense of rebirth.

"Ready?" Jennifer asked, her suitcase in hand.

"More than ever," Killian replied, taking her hand in his.

Together, they stepped out of their home, embarking on a new journey of love and commitment. As the door closed behind them, Killian knew that he had found peace, a resolution to the conflict that once consumed him. His heart belonged wholly to Jennifer and their children, and with that knowledge, he was finally able to move forward, leaving the bittersweet memories of his past life behind.

Chapter 13

Sharing the Gift

As the days and months went on, Killian studied and matured his ability to reach into his consciousness and learn from the elders that helped guide him between his world with Lindsay and Jennifer. Looking for encouragement from Jennifer, Killian sought acceptance with his abilities and how he could share it with others to help them understand the afterlife better so that they could find a similar peace that he had.

The mid-morning sun filtered through the lace curtains, casting shadows across the worn wooden floor of the Flaherty's living room. Jennifer sat on the edge of the white linen couch, her hands clasped tightly around a steaming cup of tea, the steam rising into the light-filled air. Killian stood by the window, staring out at the quiet neighborhood street, his forehead creased with worry and uncertainty.

"Jennifer," he began hesitantly, "I know this is difficult for you to understand. I'm struggling with it myself. But these visions...they feel real."

Jennifer took a slow, steadying breath as she considered her husband's words. She had always been a rock for him, unwavering in her support, but this new revelation was testing the limits of her trust. She shifted in her seat, tugging at a loose thread on her faded jeans, a thoughtful expression playing across her face. "Killian," she finally said, her voice soft but firm, "you're my partner and my best friend. If this is something important to you, I want to be there for you, just like you've always been there for me."

"Thank you, Jennifer." Killian's shoulders relaxed slightly, the tension easing from his body as he turned to face her. "But how do we even begin to share this with our family and friends? They'll think I've gone mad."

"Perhaps," Jennifer mused, setting her teacup down on the coffee table, "we could start by having a small gathering here at home, something informal, where we can introduce your abilities without any pressure or expectations."

"All right," Killian agreed, nodding his head thoughtfully. "We could invite everyone over for a barbecue next weekend. Keep it casual, like you said, and then, if they're receptive, I can try to share my experiences with them."

"Perfect." Jennifer smiled, her resolve fortifying as she began to mentally plan the logistics of their gathering. "I'll call everyone and make sure they can come. You just focus on preparing yourself for the big reveal."

Killian took a deep breath, his heart swelling with gratitude at Jennifer's unwavering support. He knew that this journey would not be easy, but with her by his side, he felt ready to face whatever challenges lay ahead.

"Thank you, Jennifer," he said softly, crossing the room to envelop her in a warm embrace. "I don't know what I'd do without you."

"Neither do I," she whispered back, her arms tightening around him. "But we'll get through this together, just like we always have."

As they stood there, wrapped in each other's arms, the sun continued to stream through the curtains, bathing the room in a warm golden light that seemed to promise a brighter future, one filled with love, understanding, and the unbreakable bond between two souls who had chosen to walk through life hand in hand.

As the day of the big reveal came, Killian became more nervous about what the day had in store. The scent of freshly mown grass and blooming flowers filled the air as laughter and excited chatter of children echoed throughout his backyard. Killian stood near the deck, taking in the sights and sounds that surrounded him. His chest tightened with anticipation as he watched his family members arrive one by one, their faces alight with smiles and warm embraces.

"Deep breaths, Killian," Jennifer whispered in his ear, her hand resting reassuringly on his arm. "Remember, they're here because they love you and want to support you."

Killian nodded, his eyes misting over as he took in the sight before him. Cousins, aunts, uncles, nieces, and nephews all gathered, eager to spend time with one another. It was a testament to the strength of their family bond, a bond he hoped would only grow stronger after today.

"Okay, everyone!" Jennifer called out, clapping her hands to gather their attention. "Let's get settled around the picnic tables. Killian has something special he'd like to share with all of you."

As the family took their seats, Killian found himself scanning their faces, each one etched with curiosity and genuine concern. He could feel the weight of their gazes upon him, heavy with expectation.

"Thank you all for coming," Killian began, his voice wavering slightly. He cleared his throat, determined to find his footing. "I know this gathering is a bit different from our usual barbecues, but I'm grateful to have you all here."

He paused, taking a deep breath, and looked down at the worn wooden table, its surface scarred with the memories of countless family gatherings. The familiar grooves in the wood grounded him, reminding him of the many years of love and laughter they had shared.

"As you know, I was in a coma for some time, and recently, I've been experiencing something extraordinary," Killian continued, his voice growing stronger. "I've been having visions, vivid, profound connections to past lives and loved ones long gone."

The air seemed to shift as the family exchanged glances, a mixture of disbelief and wonder playing across their faces. Killian felt a pang of apprehension, but he pressed on, bolstered by Jennifer's unwavering support.

"Every time I dream, I'm transported to another place and time," he explained, the words tumbling out of him. "I've seen myself as a soldier in the Civil War, a farmer in medieval Europe, even a poet in ancient Greece. And in each life, there are people I recognize, people I know I've loved deeply. Most prevalent is a woman named Lindsay who has shared many of these past lives with me."

As he spoke, Killian could see the flicker of curiosity in their eyes, the questions forming on their lips. He knew that some would be skeptical, while others might be more open to the idea. But what mattered most was that they were here, willing to listen.

"Today, I want to share this journey with you," Killian said, his voice laced with determination. "I hope that, together, we can explore these connections and maybe even discover our own shared histories."

A hush fell over the crowd as they absorbed his words, the weight of the revelation settling heavily upon them. Killian looked to Jennifer, her eyes filled with pride and love, and knew that no matter how his family reacted, they would face whatever lay ahead hand in hand.

Rapture of the Sleep

"Let's begin," he whispered, inviting them all to join him on this incredible journey through time, love, and the unbreakable bonds of family.

"Are you sure you're ready?" Silas asked, emerging from the shadows. His voice was strong and steady but laced with a hint of concern.

"Ready as I'll ever be," Killian replied, turning toward the small gathering of loved ones who had come to witness this pivotal moment in his life. Their eyes bore into him, equal parts hope and apprehension.

"Then let us begin," Jennifer said, her hazel eyes shimmering like emeralds caught in the sun's final rays.

Killian squared his shoulders and stepped forward, entering the circle formed by his family. He could feel their energy swirling around him, a powerful current that fueled his determination. As he took his position in the center, he closed his eyes, focusing on the task ahead.

"Remember, my son," Silas whispered, his voice a ghostly echo carried by the wind, "trust in your abilities and the knowledge you have gained. You are ready."

Killian nodded, his heart pounding like a drum as he prepared to commence the final test. He drew a deep breath, inhaling the sweet scent of the meadow one last time before plunging into the depths of human consciousness.

The sun dipped below the horizon, and darkness enveloped the scene with the campfire providing an amber light as a spotlight for the show. But for Killian, a new world of possibilities was dawning.

A shiver raced down Killian's spine, despite the warmth of the campfire and setting sun that bathed the backyard in a golden glow. He clenched his fists, his knuckles turning white as he tried to stifle the tremor in his hands. His chest tightened, and for a moment, he felt as though he couldn't breathe.

"Are you all right?" Jennifer asked, her voice laced with concern. She stood beside him, her hand gently resting on his arm, offering support in her own subtle way.

Killian forced a smile, attempting to mask his anxiety. "Just a bit nervous," he admitted, his voice barely audible as if speaking louder would shatter the fragile calm he was desperately clinging to.

"Hey," she said softly, stepping closer and tilting her head to capture his gaze. "You've got this. You've come so far, and I know you're ready for this test."

He nodded, swallowing the lump in his throat. Jennifer's presence was both comforting and grounding, reminding him of the love and acceptance he sought to gain from his family. It was her empathic nature that had drawn him to her in the first place, and now it offered him the strength he needed to face what lay ahead.

"Thank you," Killian whispered, his eyes meeting hers—a sea of hazel that seemed to hold the promise of a brighter future. With her by his side, he felt as though he could conquer anything.

"Besides," she continued, a mischievous glint in her eye, "if you don't pass this test, I'll have to find someone else to explore the mysteries of human consciousness with. And that just won't be as fun."

"Is that a threat?" he teased, momentarily distracted from his nerves.

"More like an observation," she replied, grinning. "But either way, it should motivate you to give this your all."

"All right, all right." Killian chuckled, his heart still racing but now buoyed by a newfound determination. "I'll make sure not to disappoint you."

"Or yourself," Jennifer added, her tone shifting to one of gentle seriousness. "Remember, this is about proving to yourself what you're capable of."

He took a deep breath, releasing it slowly as he centered himself. "You're right. I can do this."

"Of course, you can," she encouraged, giving his arm a reassuring squeeze. "Now go show them what you're made of."

With a final nod, Killian turned toward the circle formed by his family, steeling himself for the challenge that awaited him. As he stepped forward, he felt the weight of their expectations pressing down upon him, but also the unwavering support of the woman who believed in him more than anyone else.

"Let's dive deeper," he said, his voice steadier than before, as he prepared to demonstrate his mastery and claim his place among those who had come before him.

The air around Killian hummed with energy as he closed his eyes, focusing on the intricate threads of human consciousness that surrounded him. He could feel the familiar warmth and love emanating from Jennifer, a steady beacon amid the tumultuous sea of thoughts and emotions swirling about the room.

"Killian," Jennifer's calm voice broke through the silence, "you may continue."

Inhaling deeply, Killian reached out with his mind, gently weaving together the delicate strands of his family's thoughts and memories. As he worked, he recalled the countless hours spent studying ancient scrolls and practicing his abilities under the watchful eyes of his mentors. Now, it was time to prove himself.

"Observe," Killian whispered, his hands moving gracefully through the air as he wove an intricate tapestry of memories and emotions. A collective gasp filled the room as vivid images began to materialize before them, a young Killian learning to walk, guided by his mother's gentle touch, and his siblings laughing together in the warmth of the setting sun, their faces flushed with joy.

"Remarkable," whispered his aunt, tears welling in her eyes as she relived moments long past.

"Indeed," agreed his eldest brother, Thomas, pride evident in his voice. "I never thought I'd see the day when our little brother would surpass us all."

"Nor did I," added his sister, Catherine, a soft smile playing at the corners of her lips. "But I couldn't be prouder of you, Killian."

As the images continued to unfold, Killian felt a swell of confidence within him. He had come so far, and now, with his family bearing witness, he was proving himself worthy of their respect and admiration. He could sense their genuine astonishment and pride, and it fueled him to push further into the depths of his abilities.

"Thank you, Killian," whispered his uncle, the stoic mask he usually wore crumbling under the weight of the memories Killian had brought forth. "You have a gift unlike any other."

As the last of the images faded, Killian opened his eyes and found himself surrounded by the beaming faces of his family. He had done it, he had demonstrated his abilities like never before and earned their admiration in the process. A warm sense of accomplishment filled him, and he knew that he had grown stronger, not just in his powers, but also in his heart.

Jennifer was right, he thought, glancing over at her smiling face. *I needed to prove this to myself, and now I have. This is only the beginning.*

The warm glow of triumph radiated from Killian's chest, spreading through his limbs and infusing every fiber of his being. He felt as though he had been unshackled from a great burden, the weight of doubt and insecurity finally lifted. Sweat glistened on his forehead, his breaths coming in deep and steady as he regained control after the intensity of the test.

"Congratulations, Killian," Jennifer said, stepping forward to embrace him. Her voice was soft and supportive, her eyes shining with pride. "You did it."

"Thank you, Jennifer," Killian replied, his voice thick with emotion. He pulled away from her embrace, his gaze lingering on her for a moment before turning back to his family. "I couldn't have done it without your help."

"Come, let's walk for a bit," Jennifer suggested, gesturing toward the lush garden that surrounded their backyard. As they strolled along the pebbled path, the fragrant scent of blooming flowers filled the air, and the sun cast shadows through the leaves overhead.

"Killian, what you accomplished today was truly remarkable," Jennifer began, her voice shaded with awe. "How did it feel, tapping into those depths within yourself?"

He paused, considering his words carefully. "It was like…breaking through a barrier I didn't even know existed," he admitted. "For so long, I've been afraid of my own potential, of the power I could wield if I pushed myself to the limits. But today, I found strength in that fear, and it allowed me to reach heights I never thought possible."

Jennifer nodded, her eyes reflecting her understanding. "It must have been quite a journey, to get to this point."

"It was," Killian agreed. "I faced countless challenges and setbacks along the way, but every time I stumbled, I learned something new about myself. And in the end, I realized that my greatest obstacle wasn't my abilities or my knowledge, it was my own self-doubt."

"Your determination is inspiring, Killian," Jennifer said, her hand gently squeezing his arm. "I'm so proud of how far you've come."

"Thank you," he replied, swallowing the lump that had formed in his throat. "You know, there were moments when I felt like giving up, when the weight of my failures seemed too heavy to bear. But then I would think of you…and somehow, I always managed to find the strength to keep going."

Jennifer's cheeks flushed with a hint of pink, and she looked away for a moment before meeting his gaze once more. "I'm glad I could be there for you, Killian. Through all the trials and tribulations, your love has been a constant source of comfort and support for me as well."

"Jennifer," Killian began, his voice hesitant but sincere. "I want you to know that no matter what the future holds, I'll always be here for you, just as you've been here for me."

"Killian," she whispered, tears glistening in her eyes as she leaned in close. Their foreheads touched, their breaths mingling in the space between them. "I have no doubt of that."

And as they stood there, wrapped in each other's embrace, the world around them seemed to fade away, leaving only the warmth of their love and the promise of an unbreakable bond between them.

In that moment, their love seemed to transcend the physical realm, transcending time and space to form an unbreakable bond that tethered their souls together. Hand in hand, they stood on the precipice of a new beginning, their hearts brimming with hope and the promise of a love that would defy all odds.

Killian studied Jennifer's face, her eyes shining like stars in the twilight sky. He had never imagined that someone could accept him so wholly and completely. The warmth of her embrace seemed to seep into his very soul, filling the cracks and crevices left by a lifetime of doubt and insecurity.

"Jennifer," he whispered, his heart thundering in his chest, "I can't tell you how much this means to me."

She smiled, brushing a stray lock of hair from his forehead. "You don't have to, Killian. Your happiness is enough for me."

As they stood there, their surroundings began to fade away, leaving only the two of them and the unspoken words that hung in the air between them. Their ancestors had once gathered to celebrate life, love, and the power that flowed through their veins. Now, Killian felt as if they were part of that legacy, a connection forged by blood and strengthened by love.

"Before today, I always felt like I was on the outside looking in," Killian confessed, his voice barely audible above the soft rustling of leaves. "But with you by my side, I finally feel like I belong."

Jennifer squeezed his hand, her touch gentle yet reassuring. "And you always will, Killian. No matter what happens, we'll face it together."

He gazed at her, the sincerity in her eyes setting his spirit ablaze. In that instant, a surge of determination coursed through him, bolstered by the unwavering support of the woman he loved.

"Then let's make a promise, right here and now," Killian declared, taking her other hand in his. "No more secrets, no more doubts. From this day forward, we stand united, for all eternity."

"Agreed," Jennifer replied softly, her eyes never leaving his. "Together, we'll forge a new path, one filled with love, understanding, and acceptance."

As the last remnants of sunlight vanished from the sky, the stone circle seemed to pulse with energy, as if acknowledging the strength of their commitment. Hand in hand, Killian and Jennifer stood at the threshold of a new timeline filled with endless possibilities.

And for the first time in his life, Killian felt truly free, unburdened by the weight of his past and propelled forward by the love that now anchored him firmly to the present. With Jennifer by his side, there was no obstacle too great, no challenge insurmountable. Together, they would conquer the world, one day at a time.

Chapter 14

Best of Both Worlds

The morning sun cast its warm embrace upon Killian's face, lending a soft glow to his graying hair as he strode purposefully toward the office building. It was a sight he had not seen in months, and it filled him with a renewed sense of determination. His heart pounded in his chest, the rhythm like an echo from a previous life, the life he had known before the coma.

"Welcome back, Killian!" His colleagues greeted him with genuine smiles as he entered the bustling workspace. Their voices were laced with relief and joy for his recovery. He returned their well-wishes with a warm smile and a nod, appreciating their kindness but eager to get back into the swing of things.

"All right, everyone," he announced, clapping his hands together. "Let's get down to business."

As the day progressed, however, Killian found himself struggling to find purpose in the mundane tasks that once occupied his time. The numbers on the screen blurred together, and the constant drone of office chatter grated on his nerves. It all seemed so insignificant compared to the vast expanse of multiple timelines that he now understood.

He leaned back in his chair, massaging his temples as his mind raced with thoughts of what could have been, what might still be, and what was forever lost in the shifting sands of time. How could he focus on spreadsheets and quarterly reports when he knew there were worlds beyond this one, each with their own stories and destinies?

As Killian returned home that evening, he stood at the edge of his driveway. The wind whispered through the trees, carrying the raw scent of the city. He closed his eyes and took a deep breath, feeling the weight of the day lift from his shoulders.

"Killian?" Jennifer's voice reached him from behind, snapping him back to reality. "What are you doing out here?"

"Taking a moment," he answered, forcing a smile. He hesitated, unsure how to articulate the turmoil within him. "It's been a long month. It's just..." he began, then trailed off, searching for words. "After everything I've experienced, it's hard to find meaning in the work I used to do. I feel like there's so much more out there, but I don't know how to access it."

Jennifer squeezed his hand reassuringly, her touch grounding him in the present moment. "I understand," she said softly. "But you have to remember that you're here for a reason, Killian. You survived. Maybe your newfound knowledge is meant to help you and others, not hold you back."

Killian mulled over her words, knowing that she was right. He needed to find a way to balance his new understanding of the world with the life he had built for himself and the responsibilities he held dear. But how?

"Maybe," he mused aloud, "it's not about finding purpose in the work itself but in the connections we make with others and the impact we can have on their lives."

Killian's worn leather shoes creaked as he walked up the driveway to his front door. He sighed heavily, the weight of exhaustion pressing down on him like an overfilled backpack. This past month had been a blur of endless meetings, unrelenting paperwork, and stifled yawns within the dimly lit office where he had once found solace in the mundane predictability of his job. Now, however, it seemed almost alien to him, a relic from a simpler time before his understanding of the world had expanded exponentially.

"Long day, Dad?" Casey's voice greeted him as he crossed the threshold into their cozy home. The scent of freshly baked bread and simmering stew enveloped him like a warm embrace, momentarily easing the tension that had settled deep within his bones.

"More like a long month," Killian replied wearily, setting his briefcase by the door and loosening his tie as if to physically distance himself from the oppressive collar of his work life. "But I'm managing."

Jennifer stepped forward, her soft hands cradling his face as she pressed a tender kiss on his lips. "You're a strong man, Killian Flaherty," she whispered against his skin. "But even strong men need a break sometimes."

He closed his eyes, savoring the momentary reprieve as her words washed over him. It was true; he needed a respite, but how could he afford one when there were still so many unanswered questions swirling around in his mind? The tentacles of multiple timelines seemed to beckon, teasing him with promises of untold wonders just beyond his grasp.

"Jen," he began hesitantly, his gaze fixed on the flickering candlelight that danced across the room. "Do you ever feel like…like maybe there's something more out there for us? Something grander than this life we've built together?"

Jennifer studied his face, her brow furrowing as she considered his question. "I think there's always more to discover, Killian," she finally replied. "But whether or not it's meant for us is another matter entirely."

He nodded, absorbing her wisdom as he had done countless times before. She was right, perhaps the key to reconciling his newfound knowledge with his old life lay not in striving for the unreachable, but in embracing the beauty of the present moment.

"Thank you, my love," Killian whispered, entwining their fingers as they settled moved into their living room together. He glanced around their humble abode, taking in the well-worn furnishings and the laughter of their children echoing through the halls. This was his world, and he would do everything in his power to protect it, even if it meant learning how to navigate the delicate balance between the ordinary and the extraordinary.

Jennifer nodded and wrapped her arms around him from behind, resting her head on his back. They stood in silence, the world around them slipping away.

"Let's go have dinner," she said eventually, her breath warm against his skin. "It's getting late."

Killian nodded and let himself be led back into the safe confines of their kitchen where the children had settled in for the nightly round of dinner conversations.

Night came quickly, and with it, Killian's anticipation grew. He had discovered as the world slept, he was granted entry to his conscientiousness realm, a secret place where Lindsay awaited him. Although Killian had chosen his life with Jennifer, he sometimes needed to return to Lindsay for comfort. Each slumbering moment offered an escape from the waking world, and though he knew that he could never truly belong there, he could not resist the lure of those stolen hours.

"Are you okay?" Jennifer asked, her voice quiet in the darkness of their bedroom. Her gaze searched his face for answers he could not give.

"Of course," Killian replied, holding her gaze steady. "Just tired."

Rapture of the Sleep

"Get some rest, then," she said softly, pressing a kiss to his cheek before turning her back to him.

His heart clenched painfully as she drifted off, leaving him alone with his thoughts. He knew that he should be content with the life he had, his beautiful wife, his three wonderful children, and their comfortable home, but the pull of the other realm was too strong. And at the heart of it all, Lindsay called to him like a siren's song that echoed through his dreams.

"Jennifer," Killian whispered as sleep finally claimed him. "I'm sorry."

The transition was seamless, as if waking from one dream into another. He blinked against the soft light of the moon, finding himself on a beach where waves crashed gently at the shore. Lindsay stood before him, her hair cascading down her shoulders like a silken waterfall, her eyes shining with love and passion.

"Killian." Lindsay stepped forward to engulf him in her embrace. "You're back."

"Of course," he whispered, burying his face in her hair. "I couldn't stay away."

Soft hues of pink and gold danced across the sky as the sun dipped below the horizon, casting a warm glow over the serene beach. The salty breeze teased at Killian's graying hair, carrying the rhythmic sound of waves crashing against the shore. It was a peaceful place, a world away from anything he had ever known. He is sitting beside Lindsay, her flowing blonde hair billowing around her like a golden halo, her, piercing eyes reflecting the ocean's depths.

"Isn't it beautiful, Killian?" Lindsay asked, her voice gentle as the sea breeze.

"Indeed, it is," he replied, his gaze drifting from the shoreline to her breathtaking beauty. His heart swelled with an inexplicable connection that transcend time and space.

"Tell me, Lindsay," he began, his voice heavy with curiosity and emotion. "Why do we keep reuniting in this coastal town? There must be a reason for it."

"Killian." She sighed, her eyes softening as she reached out to touch his weathered hand. "We are drawn here because our souls are connected. We've walked many paths together in countless lifetimes, but this place…this small coastal town represents something greater for both of us."

As her words washed over him, he felt the tides of memory rise within—fragments of lives spent with her, each one a testament to their bond. A thousand questions surged within him, threatening to overwhelm him like a riptide.

"Connected?" He echoed, trying to make sense of the emotions swirling inside him. "But how can that be? I'm a practical man. I've always been loyal to my family, to Jennifer and our children…and yet, when I'm with you, I feel as if I belong to another world entirely."

Lindsay squeezed his hand gently. "Our love transcends the rules and boundaries of a single timeline, Killian. This peaceful coastal town is our sanctuary, where we can be together without the constraints of time or expectation."

"Do you think Jennifer knows about this?" He ventured, the thought both thrilling and terrifying him.

"Jennifer knows you better than anyone else, and she loves you deeply," Lindsay said, her voice soothing his inner turmoil. "She understands that there are some things in life that cannot be explained or contained within the confines of one reality. Our love is one of those things."

As the sun dipped below the horizon, casting its final rays across the beach, Killian found himself lost in thought, trying to make sense of the love that spanned lifetimes and the complex web of emotions that bound them all together.

The rolling waves whispered sweet nothings to the shore as a gentle breeze played with the long strands of Lindsay's hair. Killian's gaze drifted across the sand and water before them, the colors of twilight bleeding into the horizon. The scent of salt and seaweed filled his senses, anchoring him to this moment, to this reality.

"Even though we've lived countless lives, our souls have always been drawn back to this place," Lindsay explained, her voice mingling with the song of the sea. "This coastal town is where both of our consciousnesses have found solace and peace, a haven from the chaos of our other timelines."

Killian eyes searching hers for answers. "But why here, Lindsay? What makes this place so special?"

"Each timeline has taught us valuable lessons about ourselves and each other," she said, her hand finding his once more. "With every life, we've grown closer, learned to love deeper, and understood the importance of cherishing the moments we share. Here, in this peaceful sanctuary, we can integrate those lessons and truly be free to live the life we've always desired."

"Free from the constraints of time?" he asked, the concept still foreign to him.

"Exactly," she replied with a warm smile. "Here, in this coastal town, we've created a space where our souls can flourish without the burdens of our pasts or the uncertainties of our futures. We can simply exist together, in harmony with one another and the world around us."

As the words sank in, Killian felt a sudden weight lift from his chest, replaced by an unfamiliar sense of tranquility. It was as if the pieces of a puzzle that had eluded him for so long were finally falling into place.

"Your journey has led you here, back to me," Lindsay continued, her eyes shimmering with unshed tears. "My journey has come to an end. My consciousness has completed its exploration of the many paths of existence, and I have chosen to make this coastal town my home. Killian. I am here to stay, forever."

"Forever?" he echoed, his heart swelling with a mix of fear and elation.

"Yes," she whispered, her eyes never leaving his. "We've found our way back to each other countless times, across multiple timelines, and now we can finally savor the love that has always bound us together."

"Is it wrong," he hesitated, swallowing hard against the lump in his throat, "to want to be here, with you, even though I have a wife and children waiting for me elsewhere?"

Lindsay reached out and placed a gentle hand on his arm, her touch electric despite its softness. "Only you can answer that question, Killian," she said quietly. "But know this: the heart is capable of loving many things, in many ways. It does not diminish one love to feel another."

As the sun dipped below the horizon, casting its final rays across the beach, Killian felt a newfound sense of peace wash over him. The past and future seemed to fade away, leaving only the present moment, where he stood hand in hand with Lindsay, their souls intertwined in the eternal dance of love.

"Can I ask you something?" Killian began, his voice barely above a whisper as they watched the last remnants of daylight vanish beneath the waves. The salty scent of the sea mingled with the sweet aroma of blossoming flowers that grew along the shoreline.

"Of course," Lindsay replied, her gaze still locked on the distant horizon but her attention fully on him.

"Is there...any possibility that Jennifer and my children could join us in this timeline? I cannot imagine leaving them behind, but I also can't deny how much I want to be here...with you."

Lindsay's face softened with understanding, and she reached out to place a reassuring hand on Killian's shoulder. "I am glad you asked, Killian. Our journey has brought us to this beautiful place, and it is only right that we share it with those we love."

"Would you truly welcome them here?" Killian questioned, his heart swelling with hope at Lindsay's words.

"Absolutely," she answered without hesitation, her eyes shining with sincerity. "When they are ready to explore the power and beauty of traversing multiple timelines, I look forward to meeting Jennifer and your children and sharing the magic of this coastal town with them. They are as much a part of your story as I am, and they deserve to find peace and happiness here, just like us."

With every word, Killian felt a warmth spreading through his chest, a comforting embrace that seemed to assure him that everything would be all right. He studied her face, noting the sincerity and kindness reflected in her eyes and couldn't help but feel a surge of gratitude toward this woman who had become such an integral part of his lives.

"Thank you, Lindsay." His grip on her hand tightened. "This means more to me than you could ever know."

"Love has a way of bringing people together, even across the vast expanse of time and space," she replied with a knowing smile. "And I truly believe that our love, and the love you share with your family, will only grow stronger here, where we are finally free to exist without the constraints of our pasts or the uncertainties of our futures."

As the twilight deepened into night, Killian's heart swelled with hope and anticipation for the life he would soon share with all that he loved, a life filled with love, laughter, and, above all else, peace.

"Killian." Lindsay's voice broke through his trance, her fingers brushing against his hand. He turned to face her, noting the softness of her features as she smiled at him. "Are you all right?"

"More than all right," he said, his eyes darting from hers back to the sea. The realization that had been gnawing at the edges of his consciousness finally solidified within him. His timelines, once separated by an insurmountable void, could now coexist in harmony, preserved in the love of these two extraordinary women. The weight of his decision, the fear of losing one life while embracing another, began to dissipate like the foam on the retreating waves.

"Isn't it incredible?" he whispered, his gaze locked on the distant horizon. "All this time I've struggled to understand why I was granted such a gift, why my consciousness was allowed to traverse these separate paths. And now—" Killian shook his head, disbelieving of his newfound clarity. "Now I see that, somehow, it was always meant to lead me here."

Lindsay squeezed his hand, her thumb tracing comforting circles on his skin. "This is where our souls have found peace, Killian, a place where we can be together, free from the constraints of time and the burdens of our pasts. But more importantly, it's a place where we can share the love that binds us all."

"Jennifer and the kids will adore this place," Killian said softly, his heart brimming with hope. "And I know they'll love you just as much as I do."

"Time will tell, my love," Lindsay replied with a gentle smile. "But for now, let's go home."

They walked hand in hand along the shoreline, their footprints erased by the tide as if to symbolize the blending of their worlds. The quaint cottage awaited them, nestled among the dunes and partially hidden by swaying sea grass. Its weathered walls spoke of simplicity and serenity, a sanctuary from the chaos that once consumed them.

As they approached the door, Killian paused, his eyes sweeping across the picturesque landscape one last time. A sense of gratitude settled within him, a quiet acknowledgment of the extraordinary journey that had brought him to this moment. With Lindsay by his side, and the promise of a future shared with those he loved most, Killian knew he had found the harmony that had eluded him for so long.

Hand in hand, they crossed the threshold, leaving behind the uncertainty and stepping into the warm embrace of their new beginning.

They spent the night wrapped in each other's arms, stealing kisses between whispered declarations of devotion. As dawn approached, Killian felt the familiar tug of reality beckoning him back, and he held Lindsay tighter, desperate to remain in her embrace just a little longer.

"Go," she urged gently, pressing her lips to his forehead. "I'll be here when you return."

"Promise?" he asked, his voice cracking with emotion.

"Always," she vowed, her fingers tracing the curve of his cheek.

With a heavy heart, Killian succumbed to the call of the waking world and left Lindsay behind, returning to the daylight existence that defined his reality.

As the sun rose, Killian stared at the ceiling, the ghost of Lindsay's touch lingering on his skin. A tear slid down his cheek, and he turned to face Jennifer, who slept peacefully beside him, unaware of his life each night as he slept.

"Forgive me," he whispered, knowing that he needed to find a way to bear the weight of two worlds.

Killian stood in front of the bathroom mirror, his hands gripping the edges of the sink. The reflection staring back at him seemed refreshed, a man at peace between two worlds. He studied the relaxed nature of his face and glistening eyes, wondering if Jennifer could see the happiness building within his heart.

"Killian?" Jennifer's voice, soft and concerned, filtered through the door. "Are you all right?"

He forced a smile onto his face, the muscles in his cheeks straining with the effort. "Yeah," he called back, his voice shaking slightly. "Just…give me a minute."

He turned the faucet on and splashed cold water onto his face, hoping to wash away the remnants of his dream world. But Lindsay lingered, her presence imprinted on his heart like a brand, revelation of his talk with Lindsay. Was it even fair to try?

"Killian, please talk to me." Jennifer appeared in the doorway. "You've been so distant lately. If there's something wrong, I want to help."

He reached out, taking her hand in his and led her to the bed. They sat down together, their shoulders barely touching. Killian swallowed hard, fighting the urge to confess his dreams and the woman who inhabited them.

Killian took a deep breath, his mind racing as he tried to gather his thoughts and find the right words to describe the profound connection he had forged with Lindsay and his desire to share that timeline with Jennifer and his children. "I have been going back to my timeline with Lindsay." He paused, seeking solace in Jennifer's unwavering gaze.

"I want us to go there together, Jen. I think it can bring us all closer and help us grow as a family and help me share these feelings I have."

"Killian," Jennifer responded, her brow creasing further as she tried to make sense of his words. "I don't quite understand, but if this is something that you truly believe in, then let's figure it out together."

Killian exhaled, relief washing over him as he felt the weight of his secret lift from his chest. Though he knew many questions still remained unanswered, he found solace in the knowledge that Jennifer would stand beside him on this journey to untangle the threads of his timelines.

"Jen," he continued, his voice trembling slightly. "I want you and the kids to see this place, this timeline with Lindsay. I think there's something important that we can learn from it, something that will bring us closer as a family."

Jennifer's grip tightened around his fingers, her eyes searching his. "How would we even do that, Killian? How would we share your timelines?"

"I don't know yet," he admitted, feeling the weight of uncertainty settle over him. "But Lindsay... she has this ability to connect with people on a deeper level. I believe that she can help guide us." His heart raced as he watched Jennifer process his words, trying to gauge her reaction.

She took a deep breath, her chest rising and falling as she considered what he was saying. "It's a lot to take in, Killian. But if you truly think this could benefit our family, then I trust you."

"Thank you, Jen," he whispered, gratitude swelling in his chest. He knew the path before them was uncharted territory but having Jennifer by his side gave him the courage to face whatever lay ahead.

About the Author

Kevin Cunningham was born and raised in an Irish Catholic family just outside of Boston in the quaint suburb of Auburndale. Throughout his childhood as the youngest son in a family of five and into his adulthood with his wife, children, and grandchildren, he developed a fascination with the conflicting interplay between spirituality and religion. These themes eventually formed the backdrop for his passion for writing. Kevin has worked in corporate America for his entire career and prides himself on applying his spiritual approach to coaching others. He has had a strong passion for storytelling his entire life, with the concept of how our conscientiousness could exist across multiple timelines always fascinating him. Through life experiences, he has translated his thoughts in his debut novel *Rapture of the Sleep*.

Printed in the USA
CPSIA information can be obtained
at www.ICGtesting.com
LVHW041928100224
771306LV00003B/327